Not Even Immortality Lasts Forever

Not Even Immortality Lasts Forever

Mostly True Stories

ED McCLANAHAN

COUNTERPOINT

Berkeley, California

Not Even Immortality Lasts Forever

Copyright © 2020 by Ed McClanahan
First hardcover edition: 2020

Frontispiece image: *Riding High* © Wesley Bates
Your Mixed-Up Father © Primitivo
Beware of Dog © Guy Mendes, used by permission

Library of Congress Cataloging-in-Publication Data
Names: McClanahan, Ed, author.
Title: Not even immortality lasts forever : mostly true stories / Ed McClanahan.
Description: First hardcover edition. | Berkeley, California : Counterpoint
  Press, [2020]
Identifiers: LCCN 2019026369 | ISBN 9781640092600 (hardcover) | ISBN
  9781640092617 (ebook)
Classification: LCC PS3563.C3397 N68 2020 | DDC 813/.54—dc23
LC record available at https://lccn.loc.gov/2019026369

Jacket design by Donna Cheng
Book design by Jordan Koluch

COUNTERPOINT
2560 Ninth Street, Suite 318
Berkeley, CA 94710
www.counterpointpress.com

Printed in the United States of America
Distributed by Publishers Group West

10 9 8 7 6 5 4 3 2 1

—And this one belongs to Jess!

How perfectly goddamned delightful it all is, to be sure.

—CHARLES CRUMB

Contents

Not Even Immortality Lasts Forever

A Work of Genius

If I hadn't believed it, I wouldn't have seen it.

—ARMADILLO, an old hippie

SIX HUNDRED FORTY-TWO. THAT'S HOW MANY CITIZENS reside in Brooksville, Kentucky, according to the most recent census (2010), and that, give or take a dozen or so, is how many lived there when I was among that happy number, throughout the prime years of my boyhood, 1937 to 1948. What with birth, death, and all the alternative, less dramatic varieties of arrival and departure, the population, with the exception of a handful of superannuated holdouts down at the Bide-A-Wee Rest Home, has only just managed to renew itself over the last eighty years or so. In Brooksville, the more things stay the same, the more they generally stay the same.

Which is not to say that nothing ever happens there. Indeed, one stifling dog day Saturday afternoon in the summer of 1947, the summer I was going on fifteen, God himself showed up in Brooksville—on a bicycle!

It had already been a pretty momentous summer. We'd

had a big dose of excitement back in the spring, when Luther "Two-Nose" Jukes, our illustrious native son, having exhibited his remarkable dual properties to great critical acclaim in carnival sideshows throughout the known world, came home after thirty years in theater and promptly dispatched one of his fellow citizens to a better world, by means of a small homemade bomb—just deserts, quoth the celebrated thespian, for a disdainful passing glance the gentleman had cast his way three decades ago.

I too had crossed one long-held aspiration off my list that epic summer, and was working feverishly on another: First, I had finally persuaded my reluctant self (against my vastly better judgment) to climb the water tower, the highest perch in all of Bracken County—a hundred vertiginous, heart-stopping feet straight up a silver-painted steel ladder into the midnight moonlight, a test of manly mettle among my imprudent peers, one I'd been apprehensively postponing since my going-on-twelve summer. And second, on two separate occasions I had almost mastered the intricacies of the back clasp on Big Ruthie Clapsaddle's b'zeer. (Okay, I guess it goes without saying that Ruthie Clapsaddle wasn't her real name. But she *was* big, and she *did* call it her b'zeer, as in "If you don't quit messin' with my b'zeer, mister, I'll smack the lips offa you!") So far, Big Ruthie hadn't followed through on the threat, but it had been an eventful season nonetheless; all it lacked was God on a bicycle. Coming right up.

Saturdays in Brooksville, as in most rural market towns, were festive, neighborly affairs, miniature holidays, especially so in the first years after the War, when the boys were getting back into the traces and local commerce was finally stirring from its wartime lethargy, showing signs of life. All Saturday morning, country people would be drifting into town from every corner of the county, and by afternoon the cash registers would be ringing merrily, the population swollen to half again its normal size, the sidewalks spilling into the streets, the town square clotted with humanity and humidity, the very atmosphere flush with possibility, as if something wonderful might be impending. And sure enough, on that particular Saturday in 1947, something was.

The Lord of Hosts didn't actually arrive on a bicycle, nor yet in a golden chariot descended from cerulean heavens; rather, he came by way of Route 10 out of the south from Powersville, aboard an equally preposterous conveyance, an ancient T-Model Ford flatbed truck that bore on its back a rickety-looking wooden shanty not much bigger than a chicken coop or a two-seater outhouse, sheathed in redbrick tar paper, with a crooked stovepipe poking through the roof as though it were a cartoon of itself, a stray from Snuffy Smith's herd of rolling stock. Above the cab, scrawled across the tar paper in white paint like a destination manifest, was the enigmatic admonition "HARE COME KRAMER," the letters crooked and ill-made, bleeding white.

Ah-oo-gah horn squawking insistently, the old four-banger waddled through the foot traffic in the town square and shuddered to a stop in the middle of the street, across from the county courthouse—at what happened to be the very moment I was being summarily expelled from Day's Drugs & Sundries, where for the last hour I'd been comfortably encamped in the back booth, reading comic books in the cool column of air beneath the ceiling fan, till Burnham Day discovered me and strongly suggested that I take my business elsewhere. My adolescent dignity sorely affronted, I slouched out into the muggy torpor of the afternoon and, just as the screen door slapped shut behind me, there it came, limping along like the punch line of one of the lame, unhygienic jokes I was so excessively fond of in those days, sure enough, there came a brick outhouse up the road!

The truck heaved a geriatric sigh of relief and came to rest directly across the street. On its near side, crudely rendered by the same hand in the same drippy white paint, was another iteration of the name KRAMER in large, ungainly letters. The sidewalk radiated heat like a floor furnace. I joined the growing rank of gawkers lining the curb; it was pretty easy to draw a crowd on a Saturday afternoon in Brooksville.

There were two people in the truck. A spry, sprightly old gent—Kramer himself, presumably—sporting a full head of iron-gray hair and an abundant crop of chin whiskers, shirtless and sinewy beneath his bib overalls, hopped out from behind the wheel and hastened to the rear of the rig, where he lowered a narrow ramp to the pavement, then scampered up it and disappeared inside. Meanwhile, his passenger—Mrs. Kramer, we'll assume—a stout lady in a dark, old-fashioned, ankle-length dress, with a long, pewter-colored braid coiled atop her head like the finial on an antique teapot, was ponderously making her own way to the back. There she faced the gathering crowd and stood waiting, implacable as a cigar store Indian. A moment later her energetic companion popped out like a cuckoo and handed down a bulky object and popped back in again.

The bulky object proved to be what was called, indelicately, a monkey organ, an organ grinder's music box (minus the monkey) with a shoulder strap, a hand crank on one end, and a wheezy voice like a strangling accordion. The box was cumbrous, and looked heavy, but the winsome Mrs. Kramer, nothing daunted, unceremoniously strapped it on and began grinding away, upon which the monkey organ coughed up the opening notes of "Yankee Doodle," and right on cue some hidden mechanism inside the outhouse-on-wheels simultaneously propelled the redoubtable Kramer out of its backside and down the ramp astride a silver bicycle!

Now a bewhiskered old duffer on a bicycle would have been an arresting sight all by itself on the streets of Brooksville; around there, as a general rule, bikes were the exclusive province of us aspiring juvenile delinquents, no gurls or geezers need apply. But this particular geezer was already riding around and around in the middle of the street, conducting Mrs. Kramer's rendition of "Yankee Doodle" like a bandleader! With both hands! And then—picture this—he stands up on the pedals and yanks the handlebars free and holds them aloft as if he's steering above his head and keeps right on circling with nary a wobble, describing a tight little doughnut hole amid the burgeoning crowd even as he puts the handlebars back in place and somehow manages to twist himself around, boneless as the India Rubber Man, so he's riding sidesaddle, then he's riding *backwards*, now he twists frontwards again and—still circling, remember, circling and circling—pokes his legs straight out before him and lowers his torso until he's actually pedaling with his *ass*, see, and then in one superhuman motion he levitates himself back onto the saddle and rears the bike bolt upright on its hind wheel and reaches out and magically detaches the whole front fork, wheel and handlebars and all, and presto, it's a goddamn unicycle! He tosses the now-superfluous parts aside, and around and around he flies, grinning toothlessly through his whiskers like the original foxy grandpa, this mercurial old wizard on his silver wheel with his silvery mane flowing and his arms outstretched as though he's blessing us—each time he passes, a tiny breeze cools my sweating brow—swooping and circling like some ecstatic white-crested ornithological phenomenon, a sudden commotion in the air that Brooksville might've conjured up out of its own stifling, overheated boredom, a figment of the civic imagination come bodily among us to perform uncanny kinetic miracles of equilibrium and grace and strength before our very eyes, all to the tune of "Yankee Doodle."

And that was just for openers. The doughty Kramer soon rode the unicycle back into the caravan and rode out again an eyeblink later on a velocipede, one of those Gay '90s pennyfarthing bikes with the big front wheel, astraddle which he successfully undertook such implausible activities as backpedaling and skipping rope and, I don't know, dancing the mazurka or something, all while Mrs. Kramer Yankee Doodled relentlessly—that being the only tune, it seemed, in the monkey organ's repertoire. At the edge of the courthouse square the street sloped off down a little hill, and Kramer, for his grand finale, somehow contrived to get to his feet on the saddle of the velocipede and coast all the way down to Pinck-ard's Grocery standing at military attention. As he passed the courthouse flagpole he patriotically tipped Old Glory a snappy salute, and I along with half the citizenry of Bracken County cheered lustily behind him. Moments later he was back among us, passing the hat while Mrs. Kramer expertly stowed away the monkey organ and the spare bicycle parts, and within a very few minutes the intrepid old truck was putt-putting its way out of town, toddling along like the Toonerville Trolley, headed for Maysville, the next stop up the line.

It was the first time I'd witnessed true, unadulterated genius with my own fourteen-year-old eyes. I had no name for it then, of course, but now, looking back on Kramer's performance from the perspective of the ensuing going-on-seventy years, "genius" seems about right. I would see it again only a year later, when my dad took me to a Cincinnati Reds game, and Ewell Blackwell pitched a no-hitter; and thanks to an undeservedly lengthy subsequent lifetime spent in the frequent company of writers, artists, and musicians, I've seen consummate mastery at work—art in the making—a providential number of times since then. But in my experience Kramer set the mark, and all the rest, starting with Ewell Blackwell, have had to come up to it.

Which is why I've been talking about it ever since. In those seven decades I've recounted Kramer's wondrous exploits times beyond number, to family, friends, and all manner of other captive audiences (cab drivers, dinner party guests, plumbers with their heads under the kitchen sink), especially to the creative writing classes I used to teach, where I often told it as an example of a story I fully intended to write … one of these days. Naturally, over the course of all those tellings and re-tellings, the story took on something of a life of its own, as stories will (or at any rate as my stories always do), and gathered unto itself certain adjustments, embellishments, flourishes, and adornments, to the point that eventually I wasn't quite sure I still recognized it myself. Over the years— and the re-tellings—Kramer gradually came to look less like Pappy Yokum and more like an Old Testament prophet, while his transportation slowly morphed from a jalopy to a horse-drawn gypsy caravan (complete with Mrs. Kramer as a voluptuous gypsy houri) all the way to a Conestoga wagon … and back again. Not too many years ago, remembering Anthony Quinn's rig in *La Strada*, I even wrote (and quickly abandoned) a few paragraphs positing a burly Kramer who comes roaring into town on a three-wheeled motorcycle, with a little privy-shaped accommodation for his bikes and the madam tacked on behind somehow.

As Kramer's brief manifestation in Brooksville slowly receded into deep history, his performance had seemed ever more dreamlike and evanescent, almost as if it hadn't really happened at all, as if his coming had been a visitation from some other reality, a passing fancy, an illusion. But somehow the name "Kramer" had stayed with me, and I could still vouch for the white beard and the take-apart bicycle—even the dancing velocipede—and I was still satisfied that there had been a woman with him and that she had provided some sort of musical accompaniment; but beyond that, for all I could recall, she might've played the slide trombone. Not that any of that really mattered; it was just a cocktail hour story, after all, subject to emendation as circumstances required—"because sometimes," as my West Virginia writer friend Chuck Kinder liked to say, "you just have to go where the story takes you." Nonetheless, I decided to avail myself of one more shot at finally nailing my elusive story down—at fixing it permanently, as best I could, in writing. I would dredge up every detail, I told myself, every quasi-reliable detail I could find in the cluttered storehouse of my memory, and then I'd fill in the blanks by re-creating the context, resolutely dumping the more fanciful trappings that had long ornamented my old anecdote—Farewell, tantalizing gypsy houri! Adios, Old Testament Charlton Heston-look-alike prophet!—hoping that in the process, something a little closer to the real experience would perhaps emerge. Thus resolved, I undertook to write this very story you are reading at the present moment.

So in the fullness of time it came to pass that, just as I was polishing off that passage a few paragraphs back about Kramer and his velocipede (yes, I'm a slow writer, but only because I keep interrupting myself this way), another old friend, KC in California (they're everywhere! they're everywhere!), happened across a little video on YouTube, a two-minute clip from an early-1950s movie newsreel featuring a seventy-six-year-old trick bicyclist—a *bearded* bicyclist!—who traveled the Appalachian back roads during the 1940s and '50s, performing in the streets wherever he could draw a crowd. KC, a grizzled veteran of my cocktail hour stories, recognized it and sent me a link, and suddenly, right there on my computer screen in glorious black and white was a bearded old bird by the name

of—yes!—Kramer, Harry Kramer, circling madly not on a
unicycle nor yet a velocipede but a goddamn wagon wheel!
How could I have forgotten the wagon wheel? Old Harry was
riding a ... but hey, don't take my word for it, just Google "Bicycle Tricks of the 1950s" and see for yourself, see which parts
I got right and which I was obliged to ... reimagine, as it were.
All things considered, I think I did pretty well:

Wagon wheel to the contrary notwithstanding, I found
that I'd got the venerable Kramer (alas, as of this writing he'd
be six years my junior) and most of his stunts down cold; and
in real life he certainly bore a lot more resemblance to Snuffy
Smith than he ever did to Charlton Heston, so in paring him
back down to size, I had delivered on that one as well. Because the newsreel was shot in Kramer's hometown in South
Carolina, his road vehicle doesn't appear on screen; but I'm
quite sure—well, pretty sure—that I distinctly (well, pretty
distinctly) remember an ancient flatbed with a shanty on its
back ... although I will admit that the tar paper brick is a bit
of an authorial home improvement project. Mrs. Kramer evidently failed her screen test, because she too is a no-show in
the newsreel (though her existence, to my relief, is confirmed
in the narrator's jokey voice-over: "Harry says the only thing
he can't balance is his wife's checkbook!"), so I can also con-
fess that my Mrs. K. is modeled on Miz Loweezy, Snuffy
Smith's formidable spouse. Try as I might, I couldn't quite
picture Loweezy playing the slide trombone, so I went with
the monkey organ instead. And finally, I myself impulsively
contributed Kramer's salute to the flag on behalf of both of us,
as a patriotic gesture.

I was of course thrilled to know that the great Harry Kramer's superhuman acrobatics weren't, as I'd long supposed, lost forever in the mists of time, and it was nice to have indisputable evidence that I didn't make the whole thing up. Yet for that very reason, watching the film clip was at first vaguely disturbing, like seeing a ghost. I'd been telling my Kramer story for so long, I think, that I'd unconsciously taken a proprietary interest in it, as if it existed only because I was still here to tell it. That fate had brought such luminous genius to little old benighted Brooksville had seemed to me altogether miraculous at the time—God on a bicycle, if you will—and I had long ago appointed myself his sole apostle. Once upon a time, friends, I *owned* this story—and now it's all over the goddamn Internet! Once it had been mine alone, but that was then and this is now, and I'm no longer the keeper of the flame. My work is done. Except, of course, it isn't. Kramer's passage through Brooksville had been as fleeting and ephemeral— and, in that sweltering August afternoon, as refreshing—as an April zephyr, but it would stay with me forever. The YouTube clip is just a flickering shadow; film or no film, I can still see the whole scene perfectly with my going-on-fifteen-year-old eyes. This is *my* movie now; and in this movie, Harry Kramer is still perched up there, godlike astride his giant silver-dollar wheel, cavorting in the courthouse square, his grizzled mane a wild, pale nimbus around his whiskery old mug, his arms upraised in hallelujah exultation, rejoicing in the madcap antics of his calling.

I had struck just such a celebratory pose myself a few weeks back, standing safely (whew!) on the water tower catwalk, all a-tremble with sweet relief. But the attentive reader (wake up, you slug!) may recall that I had begun that summer with two great aspirations, of which climbing the water tower was the lesser. Now the other, far more ambitious undertaking loomed before me, but my hopes were high, for with Kramer as my inspiration and exemplar, I knew full well that anything is possible. Accordingly, deep into the still-lukewarm evening of the overheated Saturday of Kramer's coming, in the course of certain rather sweaty exertions on Leo Clapsaddle's squeaky front porch glider, as heat lightning flickered and distant thunder rumbled, I untangled the Gordian mysteries of the amiable Miss Clapsaddle's hitherto impregnable b'zeer, and found within that fabled silken redoubt a muchness beyond my wildest dreams. Well, almost beyond.

Later, ambling home half drunk on the redolence of Ruthie's Juicy Fruit perfume, my hands fairly glowing in the dark with the memory of the trackless natural wonderland they had just been allowed to map, my brain aswirl with images of vast, freckle-bedappled, pink-tinged snowfields (mental Polaroids I'd snapped each time the lightning flashed—and this was before Polaroids had even been invented!), I would lift my eyes to the fulminating heavens in praise of wretched excess, and plenty of it.

And even as I write this final line, somewhere—this is *my* movie now, I'll remind you—somewhere out there in the void an invisible hand turns the crank, and while the curtain closes and the screen fades to black, an unseen monkey organ blares "Yankee Doodle" with all the gusto of the Mighty Wurlitzer.

Hatchling of the *Chickasaw*

I. *Kamp Kadet*

By the summer of 1943, my dad, the striving young Standard Oil distributor of rural Bracken County, Kentucky, had recently become a thirty-five-year-old draftee in the United States Army, and my mom, already the chief clerk of the Bracken County rationing board, was obliged to take on the stewardship of the little Standard Oil biz as well. With two full-time jobs, what she didn't need was my pudgy, myopic, probably sulky ten-year-old self underfoot all summer long, which is how I too came to get drafted—for six delightfully martial weeks of counting cadence at Kamp Kadet, a summer camp near Versailles, Kentucky, operated by a local military academy.

My dad hated the United States Army, and I hated Kamp Kadet—and for the record, our mutual distaste for our respective boot camp ordeals that summer was probably the closest he and I ever came to seeing eye to eye about *anything*.

Actually, Kamp Kadet itself was a rather nice place: a cluster of four or five modest one-story frame buildings nestled among the willow trees and sycamores on the shady, sandy banks of the Kentucky River, a picturesque, clean (in those days), mostly navigable little stream that has its headwaters down in the mountains of Eastern Kentucky and meanders northward across the state all the way up to Carrollton, where it empties into the Ohio. Behind Kamp Kadet was a broad bottomland meadow that accommodated a good softball diamond, a running track, and a little archery range. Actually not a bad place at all—if it hadn't been for Captain Batts.

During the regular school year, Captain Batts was the headmaster of the military academy's elementary school; in the summertime, he ran the show at Kamp Kadet. I never figured out whether he was a real captain, but he sure knew how to strut around like one, him in his goddamn jodhpurs and riding boots, counting cadence on the noggin of any little boy within reach with the ivory handle of his ever-present riding crop. There wasn't a horse anywhere on the property, of course; Captain Batts—Cap'n Batshit, as we inevitably named him—just liked the figure he cut in that getup. He was a handsome, vain, crewcut martinet who took a pervert's ugly delight in dominating and browbeating and generally smacking around a helpless little troop of preadolescent boys, who roundly hated him for these attentions. And in company with my fellow unhappy kampers, my distaste for Cap'n Batshit logically extended to Kamp Kadet as well, nice place that it indisputably was.

Well, my dad and I both survived that summer of our mutual discontent and many more besides, and the military summer of '43 faded into distant memory, no doubt for both of us. A lot changed over the ensuing fifteen years, but none of it stopped the clock, so that by the early summer of 1958, I had somehow morphed into a newlywed, newly minted master of the arts in English, reluctant courtesy of the University of Kentucky, where I hadn't done well—indeed where, as a matter of incontrovertible fact, I had flunked the master's oral exam, and where, alas, I'd had to trudge through yet another tedious academic year before I became eligible to try again. Including the two academic quarters I'd spent flunking out of grad school at Stanford in 1955–56, it had taken me three full years to get what was surely the lamest MA ever relinquished by the UK English department.

Now during those same fifteen years my father's circumstances had also changed dramatically, in his case very much for the better. His Standard Oil business had expanded to include the adjoining county, and we had moved to Maysville, a bustling, prosperous Ohio River town twenty miles to the east. In 1948, a Standard Oil Company towboat, pushing a tow of petroleum-product barges on the Ohio, caught fire and sank, stranding the mighty Standard Oil Company of Kentucky's river transportation system high and dry. (A towboat, for some obscure nautical reason, doesn't tow barges, it pushes them; and by the same peculiar logic, the string of barges that the towboat pushes is called ... a tow!) My father, who had an exceptionally sharp eye for the main chance, quickly partnered up with another sharp-eyed Standard Oil agent named Pete, and together they scoured the Ohio River dockyards until they turned up an antiquated but sturdy little out-of-work sternwheeler named the *Chickasaw*. They took in another

partner, formed a little company of their own—Triangle
Towing—leased the *Chickasaw* on the cheap, rounded up a
pilot and a crew, and started moving product on the Ohio between Pittsburgh and Paducah for Standard Oil.

The *Chickasaw* soon proved herself up to the task, and
the Triangle partners prospered accordingly. (And I must
say I'm damned glad they did, considering that this particular hatchling of the *Chickasaw*—namely me—has lived for
many years mostly on the proceeds of a trust fund that had
its inception in the earnings of that unlovely but lovable old
tub, bless her heart.) When they'd raised sufficient capital, the
partners bought the hardworking old gal outright, and for the
next five years or so she paddled tirelessly back and forth in
their service, pushing tows of six or eight petroleum barges—
immense floating steel vaults, each with a deck the size of
two high school basketball courts laid end to end—plying the
Ohio between Pittsburgh and Paducah. Triangle, meanwhile,
began accumulating a little string of barges unto itself, which
the partners leased to Standard Oil—whose executives they
simultaneously showered with country hams, cases of Old
Charter whiskey, Harris Tweed sport coats, football tickets,
and similar wampum, in return for which those wily emi-
nences generously condescended to include Triangle's barges
in the *Chickasaw*'s tow—meaning that the Standard Oil Company, unbeknownst to its oblivious stockholders, would be
paying the Triangle Towing Company untold thousands for
moving its—Triangle's!—own barges!

Which, judging from today's headlines about Wall Street
chicanery, is more or less how most big and wanna-git-big

business is conducted to this very day ... and always has been. But I digress.

So by dint of this and many similar stratagems over the years, my dad and his partners did very well indeed. Eventually, they replaced the *Chickasaw* with a larger, more up-to-date towboat, the fortuitously named *City of Maysville*, and then they added the still larger *Elisha Wood* and a couple more barges to their burgeoning little navy, and began working for Ashland Oil and Gulf Oil as well as for Standard. Somewhere along the way, my dad bought a summer cottage on a remote local lake, and the purchase included a big red wooden canoe, another addition to the fleet. (In the late summer of 1958, my grad student friend Wendell and I would take a glorious four-day trip down the Kentucky River in that canoe, an adventure that cemented a friendship that has lasted, now, for more than sixty years.) Then, in the spring of 1958, my dad ponied up big-time for his own personal flagship, a brand-new, ostentatiously bulky, embarrassingly overpowered houseboat, for which he proposed to stage a gala launching party at—of all the spots he could have chosen on all the countless miles of riverbanks and lakeshores in the whole state of Kentucky— Kamp Fucking Kadet!

II. Little Sir Puny Takes a Dip

My father, Eddie (Edward Leroy, officially), was born and raised—or, as they liked to say around there, "reared"—on a rocky little hillside tobacco farm in a rural community called Johnsville in Bracken County, Kentucky, about fifty miles east of Cincinnati, within a couple of miles of the Ohio River. As a boy, he swam and fished in the Ohio in the summertime, and even crossed it on the ice a few times, in bad winters. My mother, Jessie Poage, grew up in Brooksville, the county seat. During my parents' courtship, she was a schoolteacher in Neville, Ohio, to which she commuted via the mailman's rowboat. I was born in Brooksville, but we soon moved a few miles north to Augusta, a river town. My earliest clear memory is of moving out of our house in Augusta during the flood of 1937 ... in a rowboat. I was five years old, and I had the chicken pox. We three wretched refugees—Eddie and Jessie and this meager, itchy little fellow they called "Sonny"—disembarked at the first opportunity and headed for the hills, meaning Brooksville, the highest point of ground in Bracken County, where we stayed for the next eleven years, high and dry.

But the Ohio was never far away. Sometime around 1940, my dad and his brother Don and their cousin Charlie had partnered up with a jackleg carpenter named Punch Vermillion and built a little fishing camp (maybe the world's first timeshare) on the riverbank at Bradford, near Augusta, fifteen miles or so from Brooksville, and my folks and I and the other partners and their families spent great chunks of our summers there during most of the 1940s (of course excepting, insofar as both my father and I were concerned, that miserable military summer of '43). It was my favorite place under heaven.

The setting, come to think of it, was very much like that of Kamp Kadet: a broad river bottom, a sandy riverbank overhung with great, grieving willow trees, a serene river flowing before them like a benediction. Our camp was a humble four-room board-and-batten ensquatment beneath the lowering canopy of willows. No electricity, no running water; we had a privy out back in the cornfield (during the war, it became a hemp-field) and an icebox and a kerosene cookstove and kerosene lamps, and the grown-ups hauled drinking water and ice from town once a day. The building itself was basically just a shell, a big tin-roofed wooden tent on stilts, the riverbank sloping away beneath it. There were two large sleeping rooms (one for gents, one for ladies), each with a couple of iron bedsteads and two or three iron bunkbeds and half a dozen cots (all available on a first-come, first-served basis), a kitchen featuring the aforementioned appliances plus a vast array of cast-iron skillets and cast-off crockery and tableware, and a long screened-in porch that stretched all the way across the front of the building and accommodated a huge, rough-hewn picnic table and two long benches. Each room had its own screen door (to facilitate access to the privy, whose irresistible appeal kept the screen doors slamming day and night), and all the windows were screened as well, so that, in the sweltering Ohio Valley summertime, our camp had the best—indeed the only—air conditioning in Bracken County.

There were always lots of kids to run with; cousins and second cousins abounded, in company with the numerous spawn of the prolific Punch Vermillion. The cousins were mostly okay, but older, and pretty much inclined to ignore me. I tended to be puny anyhow, so that left me easy prey for the Vermillions, a pack of bloodthirsty urchins who terrorized me for most of the first couple of summers we went camping there. Sometimes I brought along one or another of my small-fry Brooksville homies, in the vain hope that they'd stand with me against the teeming Vermillions, but the treacherous little ingrates all too often went over to the enemy. Which meant, unhappily, that the ranks of the punies were usually reduced to one, namely me, Little Sir Puny, and also that even though I was at my favorite place under heaven, I was often in utter, abject misery the whole time I was there.

That all changed the summer I was eight—1941—when I learned to swim there, the hard way: My dad took me out in a rowboat and pitched me in the river. Tough love, sink-or-swim variety. I resented the hell out of it at the time, and I still do. Nonetheless I did make it to shore, sputtering and bawling, and, *mirabile dictu*, from that day forward I could swim! I was no Johnny Weissmuller, granted, but I never drowned once.

Now here's an odd but salient fact about country kids in those days: By and large, we couldn't swim. Girls hardly ever even tried (it wasn't quite proper), and for most farm boys the only waterholes available were shallow creeks and farm ponds, fine for paddling around in but not so good for actual swimming. Hardly any of the smaller towns had municipal pools, and private pools were an unthinkable luxury; from Brooksville, the nearest swimming pool was in the next county, twenty miles away. (My mother and her seven siblings all grew up in Brooksville, and none of them could swim a lick, although one of my heftier aunts could float like an empty barrel.) Unless you lived near the Ohio, you'd have had to jump down a cistern or stick your head in a horse trough to find water in Bracken County deep enough to drown in. Wading and dog-paddling were the aquatic engines of choice.

Although I don't suppose my father ever saw a Tarzan movie in his life—he didn't have much use for movies—his swimming style surely owed something to Johnny Weissmuller. Alone among the men his age of my acquaintance, my dad employed an overarm stroke and a flutter kick; a crawl. He gently rolled his shoulders with each stroke, and elegantly flicked his hands—feathered his oars, so to speak—instead of flailing at the water like a human paddle wheel. Unlike Tarzan, he steadfastly kept his face above the surface, rigidly fixed on the immediate future, as though he were his own figurehead. (I regarded this little idiosyncrasy as my father's personal refinement of Tarzan's technique, and marveled that Johnny Weissmuller hadn't adopted it himself, if only just to guarantee that he wouldn't run head-on into a crocodile.) I have no idea where my dad learned to swim that way—his older brother, Don, was a wader all his life—but locally the style was very distinctive, and he was widely admired thereabouts as an aquatic phenomenon.

Intuitively, I understood these developments perfectly well even before my dad pitched me in the river. Okay, I'm cheating here a little bit: in fact, he gave me a couple of rudimentary swimming lessons, and concluded that it was time for me to try it on my own—and *then* he pitched me in the river. Anyhow, by the time I sputtered ashore, mad as a wet hatchling, I had already determined that since I was now, albeit reluctantly, forevermore a swimmer, I was by god gonna swim like Johnny goddamn Weissmuller ... and my own goddamn daddy.

(All this bad language, needless to say, is strictly retroactive. But had I been, at the time, a more accomplished blasphemer—and a whole lot braver—those are among the milder terms with which I might've expressed myself.)

Well, it took a few days, but eventually I got the overarm-and-flutter-kick business down pretty good, and I could put my face in the water too, although I never did quite figure out the breathing thing. Obviously, Johnny and my dad had each developed his own individual breathing technique, so I simply did likewise—which is to say I held my breath and shut my eyes and launched myself forward, facedown, as blindly purposeful as a torpedo, for as many highly stylized Tarzanian strokes as I could squeeze into a single breath, meanwhile flutter-kicking like a demented horizontal ballerina; I surfaced when I absolutely had to, gasped aloud as though I were drowning, then shut my eyes again and plunged ahead, crocodiles be damned.

Nonetheless, unorthodox though it was, my new mastery of the aquatic arts rendered me, as it had my father before me, the best swimmer in my age group at our camp. The adults designated me the camp junior lifeguard, which elevated my status among my juvenile campmates to unprecedented heights. A couple of years later, at Kamp Kadet, I won a Tadpole certificate signed by Cap'n Batshit himself.

Except for roller skating (I was destined to become, in the prime of my adolescence, a devilish fine roller skater), learning to swim would remain my proudest athletic accomplishment until the day, years later, when I threw an egg through the wind wing of a moving car. But that's another story, one I've told too many times already.

III. Granddad Was a Pinhooker

My father's mother, Stella Yelton McClanahan, lived to be ninety-two, and I came to know her very well, and to love her very much; my father's father, Claude McClanahan, died before I was two years old. Both the Yeltons and the McClanahans had been landowners and tobacco farmers in Bracken County, near the tiny community of Johnsville, for generations, and both families, I believe, eventually went into local commerce. "In 1884," according to a local history, "Johnsville had a hotel, a tobacco warehouse, two wagon and blacksmith shops, a dry goods store, a general merchandise store, a doctor, a justice of the peace, and a constable." My great grandfather Jonce Yelton and his business partner John Jackson (hence "Johnsville") were proprietors of the general store and post office, and I have reason to suppose (see below) that the McClanahans had gone into the dry goods line, just down (or up, or across) the road from the two "Johns'" General Merchandise & US Post Office.

I don't know much about my grandfather Claude, but I do have an 1890-vintage formal studio photograph of the Johnsville McClanahans, featuring Claude with his identical twin, Clifford—two dashing young blades as alike as department store mannequins, in matching cutaway coats and waistcoats

and high, starched collars, good-looking fellows with dupli-
cate dark, upturned mustachios and longish sideburns and
black hair parted precisely in the middle.

Unhappily, I have no idea which of the two might be
Grandfather Claude, nor of whatever became of Great-Uncle
Clifford—whichever one he is. To my knowledge, Clifford
had no progeny, nor do I recall any shirttail cousins showing
up from that branch of the slim little sapling that represents
all I know of my paternal family tree. I assume that (metaphor
alert) the Uncle Clifford twig never bore fruit.

In the family photograph, Clifford and Claude (or vice
versa) are standing behind three seated figures, a grim-
looking elderly couple—my paternal great grandparents,
presumably—and a pallid youth of seventeen or eighteen—a
nephew? cousin? redheaded stepchild?—with a rabbity, evanescent look about him, as though he too, like Uncle Clifford, were already vanishing from recorded history. (Which,
apparently, he did, without a trace; to this day, we have no
idea who he was.) The whole gloomy tableau is framed by the
studio's ponderous, funereal drapery. Nobody cracks a smile.

Now, well over a century later, I have it on good authority, handed down to me by some indescribable yet incontrovertible intra-familial telepathy system (as is the case in many
families, we didn't talk about certain things, we just *knew*
them), that throughout their long married life, Claude insisted on selecting my grandmother Stella's hats. My father
was like that too; shopping for my mother's clothes—or mine
or, best of all, his own—was among his favorite diversions.
I've even got a touch of apparel mania myself, as evidenced

by the knee-length red velvet cape I affected in the 1960s. The point here being that we McClanahans are indisputably of the dry goods denomination, on the dubious strength of which flimsy evidence I submit that my predecessors were almost certainly the proprietors of Johnsville Dry Goods, across (or down, or up) the road from the Gen. Mdse. & USPO.

I know almost nothing at all of my family's doings between the time of that photograph and 1908, when my father was born on the little farm just outside Johnsville, and very little of them thereafter until I myself came along in 1932, but it seems safe to assume that things hadn't gone all that well for the McClanaclan. As far as I can determine, the dry goods store was long gone—I'm guessing it failed in the early 1900s, during the Black Patch troubles of those years, when the tobacco market tanked—and of the five people in the photograph, by the 1920s only Claude was still sensible to the pinch, and he apparently hadn't prospered. He was the father of three—my aunt Mabel, my uncle Don, and the youngest, Eddie, my dad—and he was further burdened with "Unk," Stella's brother (another Clifford, inconveniently, so let's just stick with "Unk"), who had distinguished himself within the family by never really doing anything at all, and was a heavy feeder as well. The farm, which boasted (according to my late father's boyhood memories) the requisite good milk cow, a few beef cattle, a couple of hogs, and a garden, could have sustained the whole outfit, even when it wasn't producing much at all in the way of revenue ... But that wouldn't have supported Claude's tastes in stylish haberdashery, fine millinery for my grandma (a shy, retiring soul who would probably have worn a flowerpot on her head if her handsome husband had told her to), and, I daresay (knowing my father's predilections, and my own), a daily infusion of good whiskey if he could get it. And how in the world did he finance a year at the University of Kentucky for each of his two sons?

Well, see, he had himself a little something going on the side: he was what they called a "pinhooker"—that is to say, he was a small-time, short-term speculator in the price of leaf tobacco on its way to market, buying it in the street from cash-strapped growers and then immediately reselling it inside the sales warehouse. "These pinhookers"—sniffed a 1960 history of the tobacco industry called *Tobacco and Americans*, by Robert K. Heimann, an industry flack cum executive—"were not above scouting the leaf country and frightening farmers into distress-selling with rumors of overproduction, disappearance of important buyers from local leaf centers, and the like." Pinhooking was a costly nuisance to the buyers, a sometimes-necessary evil to the sellers—and generally considered a pretty shady calling either way you sliced it. It wasn't criminal, exactly, but (people said) it was the next thing to it.

So my family never bragged much about Grampa Claude the Pinhooker, but I like to picture him stationed outside the warehouse door, a stylish anomaly among the milling throng of tobacco farmers, tradesmen, and teamsters, spiffy and handsome in his starched collar and upturned mustachios, a boutonniere of sales contracts in his breast pocket, doing a little bidness on the side. Minus the moustache, he could be my dad.

Claude's career in pinhookery came a cropper with the

Great Depression, when everything else did likewise. His last known employment was in 1933, when my grandfather Poage, my mother's father, hired him to paint an outbuilding on his farm in Brooksville, the county seat. Both grandfathers died in 1934.

As anyone who has read my work knows to the point of distraction, my favorite characters, real and imagined, are rogues of a certain stripe—charlatans, roughnecks, pranksters, grifters, show people, writers—and I'm proud to add pinhooker to the bills of indictment, and my grandfather Claude to the roster of perpetrators and usual suspects. My hope is that Claude, rest his soul, is currently enjoying and appreciating the society of Monk McHorning and Philander Cosmo Rexroat and Little Enis the World's Greatest Left-Handed Upside-Down Guitar Player, and that they consider him an amiable and worthy addition to their ranks.

Just mention my name, Grampa, and tell 'em you're with the band.

IV. Cundoms!

My dad was also a handsome man—and don't think he didn't know it. His best feature, he felt—and rightly so—was his nose, which was indeed straight and well formed. To complement that impressive ornament, he boasted a strong brow and chin, a direct (if somewhat wary) gaze, and a fine head of dark, wavy hair; but I know for a fact that he was particularly fond of his nose, because in my childhood he was forever holding it up to me (so to speak) as an ideal that my own sorry little snoot should aspire to. The nose, my father firmly believed, is composed of certain pliable matter that one can mold and shape over time like a lump of gristly modeling clay, if—*if*—one develops the proper habits of life, and sticks to them assiduously. Such as: When said olfactory apparatus itches, son, do not scratch same by rubbing it with the heel of your hand as if you want to smear the goddamn thing all over your countenance. Rather, delicately grasp it between the thumb and forefinger, just below the bridge—thus; yes; just so—and gently pull forward and down, thereby addressing the offending itch while simultaneously helping the nose to become all that it can be, which is to say a nose not unlike the paternal beezer itself.

I'm probably exaggerating a little here, but it seemed to me that I was subjected to this lecture-cum-demonstration at least three times a day for about a thousand years, before my father finally had to accept the incontrovertible fact that we were both stuck with the nose I was born with; I'd have to wear it and he'd have to look at it, and no amount of coaxing or stroking was going to improve it. Nor did his pious sermonettes on the evils of breaking down the heels of one's shoes by never untying the laces have the desired effect; for, at the risk of eternal damnation, I willfully persisted in this irresponsible behavior as well, to such an unconscionable extent that the nice oxfords he kept buying me were regularly soon reduced to primordial leather flip-flops.

And haircuts! He was a stickler—not to say a real dick—when it came to haircuts. A good haircut, he insisted, should be invisible to the naked eye, as indiscernible as a tonsillectomy. (Never mind that looking like he hadn't had a recent haircut required him to have a *lot* of ... haircuts.) During his brief stint in the military, the close-cropped GI scalping that the US Army had inflicted on him was, in his opinion, practically a war crime; and, when he came home, the whitewalls and bowl cuts of the sort Brooksville's old-school barbers tended to administer were equally unacceptable. Eventually, he discovered a barber in the nearby town of Falmouth who had a satisfactory way with sideburns—which meant that every other Thursday he and I were obliged to travel eighteen miserable miles of crooked, upsy-downsy country road in my dad's cherished war-surplus Mercury station wagon (more on that momentarily), for the purpose of subjecting ourselves to an evanescent cosmetic procedure that would last only two weeks before it had to be refreshed. None of this made a lick of sense to me—I didn't even *have* any sideburns!—and I voiced my opinion of it in a bitter stream of whining and sulking, which he resolutely ignored until, on the third or fourth trip to Falmouth, I expressed my unhappiness more emphatically, by upchucking in the front seat of his beloved Merc. That did it, at last. From then on, he went to Falmouth by himself, and left me to the inept attentions of Brooksville's cheerfully artless barbers.

All this fussy attention to grooming may seem a bit improbable, coming as it did from a country boy from a little old backwater burg like Johnsville, but I think it merely lends credence to my theory that there's a haberdasher bottom-feeding in the McClanahan gene pool. My father set great

store by the ancient adage that clothes make the man, which,
when you think about it, is like believing that a ten-gallon hat
makes a cowboy. He had begun his Standard Oil career driving his own small tank truck, delivering gas and heating oil
and kerosene around the county, but he hired a driver to re-
place himself the very first minute the business could afford
it, sometime during my toddlerhood; and, to my knowledge,
from that day forward he never wore work clothes again.
No more greasy overalls for him, no high-water britches, no
ready-made duds from Monkey Ward! More and more often,
as he prospered, he found occasion to shop in Cincinnati or
Lexington or Louisville, where your menswear personnel understood that the cuff of the trouser ought properly to break
just so across the laces of the wing tip—the highly polished
wing tip, I should say, because my dad gave his footwear a
lustrous Willy Loman shine every single morning. Not that
he was flamboyant or dandified; he favored subdued colors—
brown and tan and beige; solids, no stripes, no racetrack
plaids—tweed sport coats, creased gabardine trousers, quiet
neckties, wide-brimmed fedoras. If there had been a contest to
name the best-dressed gent in Bracken County, he'd have won
by acclamation.

He might have done almost as well in a local popularity
contest; he was personable, and people clearly enjoyed doing
business with him. His dealers, the folks who operated little country stores and filling stations and garages all around
the county, liked him, and were loyal to him when a certain
Mr. Tuggle, of Gulf Oil, tried to horn in on his territory. Even
my dad's burgeoning wardrobe, which you'd suppose might

have met locally with a healthy dose of who-the-hell-does-he-think-he-is?, was instead considered an honorable badge of his achievements. He bought up first one, then another of Mr. Tuggle's remaining Gulf stations, and resold them both as Standard stations. He put in a lot of time in Frankfort, the state capitol, busily drinking whiskey and playing poker with politicians, while he hustled them for contracts with the state to supply product for local highway-resurfacing projects.

Meanwhile, the few months he had spent in the army, plus an even shorter stint in the merchant marines, made him a veteran in good standing, which entitled him to first dibs on war surplus stuff the government was unloading at bargain prices at a military salvage yard in Northern Kentucky, even while the war was still very much in progress. The "war effort," as it was known, had completely shut down the production of cars and trucks and even tractors for civilian consumption, and used rolling stock was at a premium. Farmers were especially hard-pressed for vehicles that could handle rough terrain, so the first thing my dad bought at the salvage yard was an army personnel carrier, a hulking, heavily armored, olive drab beast of a battlefield vehicle with a tiny slit of a windshield that made it look for all the world like a great green, squinty-eyed toad. He hired a welder to cut off the armored rear end, sold the heavy iron plates back to the government as scrap metal, hired a carpenter to build a flatbed on the back, and sold the repurposed rig to a local farmer at a tidy profit.

Next, he and a partner, a garage owner named Fred, bought a small bus that had been used by the military police to haul misbehaving GIs back and forth between the brig and their workstations, so it came with escape-proof heavy wire screens on all the windows—ideal accessories for the purpose my dad and Fred had in mind for it: within days they had leased the bus right back to the government for hauling German POWs from a nearby encampment to work in the Bracken County tobacco harvest. They made back their initial investment in a few weeks, and then, just as the tobacco season ended, one of the county school buses broke down beyond repair, so they quickly painted their olive drab bus a bright mustard yellow and leased it to the county for an emergency school bus, in which capacity it served until the war was over, inescapable windows and all. (Not to suggest that they were heartless; just that they probably never even considered the danger. No one paid much attention to vehicular safety in those days.) Finally, they painted it pale blue and sold it to a church—for more than they had paid for it three years before.

My father's favorite score at the salvage yard was the Mercury station wagon. The Merc, an elegant woody beneath its obligatory coat of olive drab, had been the official vehicle of a ranking officer. My dad took it directly to his friend Fred's body shop, where Fred's body and fender guy stripped away its grim militaristic veneer, painted the body a rich, deep maroon, and refinished and varnished the wooden panels to a high gloss. The wagon ran like a top, so for the Duration (the polite name for the ongoing horror of the war), the McClanahans had the classiest ride in Bracken County—or at least it was until I upchucked in it.

No question about it, my dad was a chip off the old pinhooker, to the manner born. Like his daddy before him, he was a speculator, inasmuch as most of his business transactions—from cars and filling stations to towboats and barges—were financed on the cuff, and were therefore speculative ventures, gambles. He told me not once but many times that he *believed* in being in debt. (He believed just as devoutly, by the way, in the certifiably insane economic strategy called "planned obsolescence.") But my dad was sharper at it than his progenitor, or perhaps just luckier; in any case, his assets grew faster than his liabilities, and once he got ahead of the game, he stayed ahead. The word "entrepreneur" wasn't yet in currency, but it would have described him perfectly. Prosperity seemed to fit him, and he wore his success like a well-tailored suit.

Like most boys growing up in tobacco country back then, my dad took up smoking when he was eleven or twelve, and was a two-pack-a-day man for the rest of his life—which, as you may already be surmising, was destined to be regrettably short. Meanwhile, however, cigarettes were as vital an accessory to his style as his Dobbs fedora or his Florsheim wing tips. Eventually—let's say by the summer of 1948, the summer I was fifteen (and counting, feverishly)—he had settled on Pall Malls, a rather hoity-toity brand, the preferred smoke (so said the advertising slogan) "Wherever Particular People Congregate." Pall Malls were the first popular "king-sized" cigarettes, only a fraction of an inch longer than regular, but by comparison they seemed as long and slim as soda straws. Sometimes, when he had an audience—in the Brooksville drugstore, say, where the not particularly "particular" folks from the courthouse across the street tended to congregate—my dad would make a stylish little dumb-show just of lighting one up. Palming his favorite Zippo, he'd produce the next impossibly long Pall Mall from his shirt pocket and sort of present it to himself with the merest hint of a flourish, giving himself a moment to anticipate the satisfaction it was about to bring him; and then he'd shoot his left cuff and, holding the long cigarette the way one holds a pencil, tamp it smartly three or four times against the crystal of his wrist watch (a Gruen Curvex with a gold expansion band) before situating the slender white wand between his lips—whereupon, with an adroit sleight-of-hand fillip of the Zippo accompanied by a sharp snap of the fingers, he somehow popped the lighter open and simultaneously sparked a blue flame that seemed to leap from his thumbnail and set the Pall Mall's tip aglow.

I was fascinated by this bit of legerdemain, at least in part because at the time I was secretly developing a raging tobacco habit of my own, on cigarettes my pal Shoobie Hamilton filched from his mom and shared with me, and I was immediately interested in anything that might hasten or enhance or foster my corruption. (Indeed, I had already appropriated one of my dad's old Zippos, and was privately trying to teach myself his drugstore stunt. My parents and I were to move to Maysville at the summer's end, and I was determined to be an accomplished smoker by the time I got there.) But my father, although he was barely forty at the time, understood all too well that he was smoking himself into an early grave (as an object lesson, he used to insist on showing me the yellow stain that cigarette smoke would leave when he blew it through a white handkerchief, the same ominous yellow that stained his fingertips), and he had already determined that it was his parental duty to ruthlessly stomp out any attempt I might make to follow in his footsteps. Thus we set the stage for three years of deceit, rancor, craven lies, and broken promises on my part, and three years of suspicion, constant vigilance, empty threats, and corrosive anger and frustration on his part.

In early July, on the grounds that he was tired of seeing me loafing around the drugstore (no matter that he only saw me when he was loafing there himself), my dad obliged me to quit my half-assed job as a skate-boy at the local roller rink, in order to take an even more half-assed job pumping gas at a new Standard Oil station he was investing a little money in, a raw-looking, sunbaked cinderblock excrescence squatting in a half-acre patch of new gravel alongside the county highway, a couple of miles out of town. The proprietor, who had built the station on a corner of the family farm, was lining up a franchise to open as a farm supply store. Red tape had slowed the process, but in deference to my dad (who fronted him the tanks and the pumps and a big Standard Oil sign, and paid for all that gravel), he had agreed to jump-start the filling station portion of the fledgling enterprise and begin pumping gas right away. My services as an indentured pump jockey, it seemed, were included in the deal.

Six days a week for the next two months I was to ride my bike out there and open the station at 7:30 in the morning, and stay till I got back on the bike and rode home at 5:30 that afternoon. The owner—I'll call him Ralph—a sporting young marine vet with a lively social life, would come in at 9:30 or 10, still sleepy-eyed and yawning, and lurk about the premises for an hour or two, checking the inventory and poking around disinterestedly until he suddenly remembered urgent business awaiting him in town, and that would often be the last I'd see of him till closing time.

There was very little traffic on the highway, and most of that was going somewhere else; sometimes as much as an hour would pass between customers. Once in a while, one or another of my adolescent running mates would ride his bike out from town to score an illicit pack of smokes from the cigarette machine, but there was nothing much to hang around for, so they generally didn't stay long. Now and then Ralph's father, a prosperous but grumpy old farmer who lived just down the road from the station, would pull his farm truck in, blowing the horn impatiently as he came, my signal to come out with a rag and wipe the tobacco juice off his side window—he kept forgetting to roll it down before he spit—while I listened to him grouse about the way certain people (meaning me) lollygag around these days. I got even with him by wiping his windshield with the same rag, and then providing the same service to his son's customers for the rest of the day.

Otherwise, I had the place pretty much all to myself a good deal of the time—not a bad gig, actually, except for the tobacco juice and the boredom factor. And I was pulling down a cool six dollars a week—yep, that's right, a dollar a day—virtually every nickel of which went, nickel by nickel, right back into Ralph's pocket, owing to my appetite for his snacks and soft drinks and especially for the fruits of that unholy cornucopia of vice, his cigarette machine, which took in thirty cents at a single gulp, and in return coughed up seductively aromatic little packages of sin and corruption.

The building was divided into two rooms, one roughly twice the size of the other. The larger room stood empty, awaiting the arrival of the still-ephemeral farm supplies; the smaller one, "the office," was my domain. But for the cigarette machine, the only furnishings in the office were a Dr Pepper soft drink cooler, a small metal desk, a few rickety metal folding chairs, and a short counter bearing a rack of candy bars and peanut butter crackers ("Nibble a Nab for a Nickel!"), along with half a dozen cans of motor oil. The decor featured a 1948 calendar displaying a busty lady mechanic in strategically unbuttoned Standard Oil coveralls; the ceiling was adorned by three or four long, dangling curls of flypaper. There was a feeble little electric fan on the desk, and a window looking out on the two gas pumps standing sentinel in the sea of gravel around them.

We also stocked another commodity, one that intrigued me almost as much as the cigarettes: For in the desk was a cash drawer with a few dollars and some small change for daily transactions, and at the back of the drawer—as I discovered the very first time I was left alone in the place long enough to venture a bit of private exploration—was a carton labeled ONE (1) GROSS SANITARY PROPHYLACTICS, and under that, SOLD FOR PREVENTION OF DISEASE ONLY. Rubbers! Or, as the more refined of my cohorts preferred to call them, cundoms! Dozens and dozens of them, each in its own matchbook-sized cardboard folder. I was momentarily jubilant at my good luck—hot damn, a king's ransom in rubbers!—until I realized that without a king to ransom, I had no earthly use for even one cundom, much less a hundred and forty-four of them. (Okay, I admit it: the folders weren't sealed, so I tried one on for size, and found its dimensions somewhat, uh, intimidating. But not to worry, friends; it went back into its little packet as good as new, and no doubt just as "sanitary" as it had ever been.) Still, I was shocked to find them there, presumably for sale, in a business in which my father was a silent partner—my father the cigarette smoker and whiskey drinker and casual blasphemer and occasional high-rolling gambler, my father who also happened to be, when the spirit moved him, a prude of Inquisitorial dimensions.

(During the ensuing years, as I metamorphosed ever so slowly into manhood, I would be reminded many times over that my dad was subject to sudden attacks of sanctimony. A chronic condition, it would keep happening even as much as ten years later—like the time he ordered my mom and my first wife and me to walk out of a San Francisco nightclub with him because a comedian was singing a song called "Go Take a Ship for Yourself.")

So was my virtuous parent aware that his associate was trafficking in impure merchandise? Or was that protected under the "Bidness Is Bidness" rubric, along with planned obsolescence? What would my virtuous mom think of this little sideline, if she knew about it? Was it okay to sell rubbers if you did it "For Prevention of Disease Only"? *What* disease? Mumps?

Well, a person with an unlimited supply of tobacco and

great chunks of time on his hands can't just sit around idly pondering existential questions, so I soon gave it up and got to work practicing my smoking moves. The station had a restroom, and the restroom had a mirror, and I whiled away long stretches of time in that dismal chamber, studying my image in the fly-specked glass with an Old Gold parked—insolently, I hoped—in the corner of my mouth, trying my best to look dangerous and antisocial. (Perversely, I had chosen Old Golds as my first brand specifically because I liked the implicit defiance in their slogan: "For a Treat Instead of a Treatment." None of your "particular people" for this aspiring juvenile delinquent!) I nearly asphyxiated myself trying to French-inhale (for the unenlightened, French inhaling is when you let the smoke roll out of your mouth even as you draw it directly up your nose; the practice was widely held to be almost indecently seductive, and I had it on the authority of a couple of very knowledgeable sophomores of my acquaintance that the very sight of a guy French-inhaling drives women wild); and in my determination to cut a fine figure when I made my upcoming debut in Maysville society, I showed that battered old Zippo no mercy as I flung it about Ralph's concrete-block bunker in clumsy attempts to master my dad's hocus-pocus.

And all that diligence paid off in the end: I never quite got the hang of the lighter trick, but on the final day of my two months of indentured lassitude, I produced the very first successful smoke ring of my life, and proudly watched it dash itself to shreds against the fly-blown mirror in Ralph's dismal restroom. *En garde,* Maysville!

V. The Honor Code

In Brooksville, I had played junior high basketball—not well, certainly (my entire three-year junior high career produced a grand total of eight points), and never with any discernible excess of enthusiasm. As a seventh grader, I had undertaken to make the team largely (I see now) as a sop to my dad, but because I manfully persisted, year by year, in getting taller just expeditiously enough to render myself an object of mild but ongoing interest to the basketball coach, I kept making the damn team despite my limitations. But the Maysville Bulldogs were recent state champions, and so confident was I that I couldn't make that team if my life depended upon it that I dutifully went out for basketball yet again, and absolutely flabbergasted myself (along with anyone who ever saw me play) by making the second string of the junior varsity. This accomplishment, such as it was, became my entrée to a whole brotherhood of surreptitious smokers: my new teammates.

Tobacco, it seemed, was to a Maysville Bulldog as hay is to a racehorse, and to the despair of our coach, an estimable gentleman named Earl D. Jones, his young stalwarts were almost unanimously devoted to it. Smokin' in the Boys Room was, of course, de rigueur, as was smokin' just about anywhere else that wasn't underwater. But Coach Jones was widely and justly revered in Maysville, and therefore he had many eyes, many Bulldog-crazed citizens who would rat you out in a heartbeat if they spotted you breaking training—even if you were, like me, an irrelevant mope at the furthermost end of the junior varsity bench. So I joined the ranks of guys skulking and slouching on the street corner outside Kilgus's Drugstore in all kinds of weather, each with his right hand cupped secretively around a smoldering fag as if we'd all been stricken simultaneously with some sort of strange digital paralysis, each of us warily scanning the passing traffic for any sign of Coach or his Argus-eyed minions ... or, in my case, for my dad's green '48 Pontiac sedan.

Inevitably, I got caught—not just once, but many times, times beyond number, and not by Coach Jones, but by my dad. Skulk and slouch as I might, the pall of guilt that descended upon me every time that accursed Pontiac hove into view must have been as obvious to my dad as the cloud of cigarette smoke around me, because again and again, I got busted.

For our first year in Maysville, my parents had rented a house on the Edgemont loop, a small suburban enclave on a narrow side road that encircles a hilltop just outside the city limits. I turned sixteen that fall, and before long I was careening around Edgemont with wild abandon at the wheel of my mother's sleek new two-door Chevy sedan, gleefully chasing our neighbors' cars off the road and across each other's lawns while my intrepid but affrighted mom, riding shotgun as my designated copilot, looked on in wide-eyed, dumbstruck terror. Nonetheless, I eventually managed to persuade her to write me an excuse from school one afternoon, so she could drive me over to Brooksville for my driver's license test—a necessity if I was to pass the test, because I still couldn't parallel park, and parallel parking hadn't yet arrived in Brooksville, where it would've been regarded as just another citified imposition.

Miraculously, I passed without incident (although the miracle was perhaps ever so slightly compromised by the fact that the young state cop who administered the test happened to be the son of an old friend of the family) and afterward, duly authorized by the sovereign state of Kentucky, I took the wheel all the way back to Maysville, eighteen glorious miles across a dream-like landscape with the Chevy's tires barely touching the pavement, a landscape intimately familiar to me, yet at the same time completely new and strange and exotic. I wasn't to see the world afresh like that again until a tab of psilocybin showed it to me in living Day-Glo in 1962. But for now, piloting that lumbering Chevy sedan back to Maysville with a brand-new driver's license in my wallet (where it was keeping company with the condom I'd boosted months ago, on my last day of work at the filling station), I was Buck Rogers at the controls of my late-model blue rocket, plying uncharted dimensions, cundom at the ready. I had slipped the surly bonds of Earth, friends, and I was outta there!

In fact, I wasn't going much of anywhere, not just yet. The next day that great green dreadnought of a Pontiac rounded Kilgus's corner just as I was copping a quick smoke with my brother Dogs, and my emancipation from the surly bonds instantly vaporized into the ether; in an all-too-apt word, I was grounded. A few days of stationary moping ensued, after which I went before the Court of Dad and entered a plea for clemency, on the grounds that I had now forsaken tobacco forever and ever, world without end—which was true enough, if you didn't count the occasional drags and still-viable butts I'd been cadging every day off my associate Bulldogs et al. to the point of becoming a public nuisance. Nonetheless, I was truly, genuinely contrite, and in deadly earnest about never, ever doing it again, no sirreebob, Judge Dad, not me.

A solemn moment, that, and a solemn pledge that lasted till I walked into the Boys Room the following morning just as Willie Gordon Ryan was leaving, and he gave me butts on the Lucky Strike he'd been about to flush. It was so delicious that at lunchtime I spent most of my lunch money for my own pack of Luckies; and I must say I particularly enjoyed the one I smoked late that same afternoon while I soloed around the Edgemont loop for the first time ever, admiring myself in the rearview mirror, me at the wheel with the Lucky hangin' on my lip, a wayward youth without (I fervently hoped) the slightest trace of character.

About six weeks later, as though I were being forced to sit through a really bad movie I'd already seen more than once, my personal toxic Joe Bltsplk cloud of commingled cigarette smoke and guilt betrayed me again on Kilgus's corner, and again I repented, and vowed to go forth (on wheels, I hoped) and smoke no more. The only difference was that this time, I wasn't all that sure I really meant it.

Needless to say, I broke that vow as readily as I had the last one. As a child, the very thought that I could lie to my parents would have been anathema to me; indeed, I couldn't have managed even the most juvenile sort of fibbery with enough moxie and conviction to get away with it. But I'd already had a few dates in the Chevy, and I fully appreciated the advantages, romance-wise, of having one's own private conveyance. In short, I had hopes and plans for that car—more hopes than plans, actually—and I absolutely could not give them up, any more than I could give up cigarettes. It was necessary, therefore, that I become a better liar or, at a minimum, that I become more comfortable while I was doing it. By the third or fourth time I got caught over the next few months, I had accomplished the latter, and was working assiduously on the former.

The more fervently I swore off smoking, the more I smoked—and, inevitably, the more I smoked, the more often I got caught. This pattern persisted like a sort of backbeat to my daily life for the next two years, an elaborate catch-and-release routine that kept playing out over and over: I'd do something cosmically stupid like, say, show up at suppertime with a pack of Luckies in my shirt pocket (They're not mine! I was just carrying them for ... uh, somebody! I don't even smoke anymore! I quit! I quit!), resulting in a life sentence of in-house custody that might last as long as three or four days, by which time my wheedling and pouting would become too annoying for my dad to put up with. On one such occasion, after he'd spent several days growling and scowling and robotically reiterating his decree that I'd never drive any car of his again ("my mom's car" was "his" too, needless to say), my dad, so bummed out by my half-baked excuses and empty promises that his exasperation blinded him to irony, tossed me his keys and ordered me to run down to the store and fetch him a pack of Pall Malls.

Nonetheless, we continued to play our respective roles in this absurd charade throughout my high school years, a protracted battle of wills in which I was completely overmatched;

my dad's will was immeasurably stronger than mine, yet in this fight he never stood a chance. For I was in the iron grip of a force that has routinely proved itself a great deal mightier than willpower: The tobacco habit, alas, had me by the short hairs, and I couldn't have quit smoking even if I'd wanted to— which, I realized after a few abject failures, I emphatically did not. Nor was it just the nicotine addiction; cigarettes had become an integral component of the image I was endeavoring to project—"brooding sensitivity, cool contempt, reckless abandon," as I once retrospectively characterized it—and I could literally no longer picture myself without them.

Meanwhile, a few weeks into fall basketball practice in my junior year, Coach Jones had mercifully put my weanling career as a Bulldog out of its tiny misery, leaving me at leisure to explore whatever extramural diversions I could find in the fleshpots of Maysville. Smoking was a high-priority item, needless to say, as was beer, which I had lately taken to with an enthusiasm that already bordered on the unseemly. Then too, there was That Other Gender, those enchanting creatures, at once so provocative and so unattainable, who occupied my every contemplative moment. I was no Casanova, certainly, and I don't intend to boast, but I was actually doing surprisingly well in that regard—meaning I could almost always persuade one or another of the unattached fascinators to let me take her to the movies and buy the popcorn. But I still had my doubts: Would they have allowed such liberties (and perhaps a few other little intimacies as well) if I hadn't had my mom's Chevy at my disposal? I didn't know—and I sure as billy hell didn't want to find out, not if I could possibly help it.

These diversions were costly, of course, and would prove
ever more so as time went on. (There was a two-dollar lady
down on Front Street who maintained a snazzy postwar Buick
Roadmaster, courtesy of a few generations of libidinous Maysville schoolboys.) I financed my revels with after-school and
summertime employment in professions varying seasonally
from hod carrier to tobacco field hand to cub reporter (at the
Maysville *Daily Independent*, where I mostly compiled thumbnail obituaries of deceased persons of no particular distinction,
who had lived—and died—in the more remote communities
in our area; the editor would never have allowed me to write
up the passing of anyone of local consequence) to surveyor's
rodman to soda jerk at Kilgus's, where I augmented my meager wages by regularly appropriating the odd pack of Luckies,
and enhanced my romantic aspirations by plying select young
ladies with fountain Cokes on the house.

My father and I carried on our epic, internecine struggle
through it all, long after my smoking was, or should have
been, a settled fact. Why he couldn't just accept that, instead
of forcing me to talk—or lie—my way out of it every time, was
a mystery to me. Why did I have to keep on quitting over and
over, when he had told me himself a thousand times that once
you start, you *can't* quit? I mean, how did that make sense?

Yet I was still getting grounded late in my senior year,
the last time just after I'd been accepted for fall enrollment
at Eustace J. Spoonbred University, a "Southern Gentlemen's"
college that prided itself extravagantly on its honor system,
whereby the student was obliged to sign a no-cheat pledge on
every exam or out-of-class assignment. (I'd also been accepted

at Miami of Ohio, where my friend Ned was already a freshman. But my dad drew the line approximately where Mason and Dixon had drawn theirs; he wasn't sending any son of his to some half-assed Buckeye excuse for a real college, when the kid could just as well go to a fine university in the heart of Dixie and learn to impersonate a Southern Gentleman.) So when I got caught smoking this time, my dad met my usual alibis and artful dodges by upping the ante: He put me on my goddamn honor! Of course I had supposedly been on my honor all along, to no discernible avail whatsoever; but now he had invoked an entire small university faculty to keep a virtual eye on me, an invisible morals squad of beady-eyed assistant professors following me around long before I'd ever set foot on their goddamn campus! My first impulse was to throw a little shit-fit at the injustice of it all—I hadn't tried that one lately—but I stifled the thought immediately when I reminded myself that the senior prom was only days away, and moreover that I had a date for the occasion with a very pretty and, I hoped, very impressionable sophomore, and, thirdly, that my mother's car—which had recently morphed (thanks to my father's devotion to planned obsolescence) into a brand-new '51 canary-yellow-and-charcoal-gray Chevy Bel Air hardtop with Powerglide and whitewalls—had an absolutely indispensable, nonnegotiable role in my plans for the evening.

Okay, hopes. My hopes for the evening.

So I squelched my objections and accepted my father's terms: on my sacred honor as an embryonic member of next fall's incoming freshman class at Eustace J. Spoonbred

University, Home of the World's Longest Concrete Footbridge, I would never fire up another cigarette, so help me
Stonewall Jackson. And that, my children, is how it came to
pass that on the following morning, as I chauffeured myself
en grand seigneur in the Bel Air to my final day of high school,
with an invisible posse of reproachful pedagogues glowering
in the backseat while I blew smoke at them in the rearview
mirror, I became the very first member of my college class to
violate the honor code.

VI. *R-a-g-g M-o-p-p*

We never got along, my dad and I; and, looking back at what
I've written here so far, I have to concede that many of my
grievances against him, taken separately, do seem rather pet-
ulant and whiney. But the little tyrannies he imposed were
equally petty and small-minded, and a dose of retrospective
whining about them may still be the only truly appropriate
response, like howling when somebody steps on your sore
toe. Meanwhile, my father's hypocrisies conveniently justi-
fied my trespasses against him, and vice versa; together, we
were a well-oiled perpetual animosity machine. We fought a
mean little war of attrition, in which each of us was his own
worst enemy, a war of which the only consequences were un-
intended ones—and finally, it wasn't even about smoking. All
that strife and struggle to resolve what, in retrospect, sounds
suspiciously like a schoolyard argument: Could a liar whip a
hypocrite?

The summer after I finished high school, my mother's youngest sister—"Aunt Pidge," we'll call her—who was a high-level secretary at the American Red Cross in Washington, DC, and also knew her way around the federal bureaucracy, lined me up with a summer job in the typing pool at the General Accounting Office, a big government agency. Pidge and Lloyd, her large, loud lout of a spouse, a traffic engineer in the Public Roads bureau, had offered to put me up for the summer in their apartment, just across the Potomac in Parkfairfax, a suburban enclave of Alexandria, Virginia, not far from the Pentagon. Lloyd had even grudgingly acceded to her suggestion that during my stay I could sometimes drive their car, a brand-new three-porthole Buick Special coupe. But he reneged on that deal right away after our first trial run through the Pentagon's Gordian snarl of cloverleaf intersections, during which I made him scream—I made a traffic engineer scream!—on three separate occasions. When we got home he snatched the Buick's keys right out of the ignition, and handed me a daily bus schedule—and to tell the whole truth, I was secretly relieved, having given myself a pretty good turn even as I was simultaneously terrifying Lloyd.

Lloyd and Pidge maintained a lively social life among their fellow cocktail-guzzling Parkfairfax neighbors, so they didn't pay much attention to my daily comings and goings. They even offered me the occasional beer when they were entertaining, and they were both unrepentant two-pack-a-day smokers who, like me, considered tobacco a vital accessory to all that was up to date and, as Pidge would've put it, "modernistic," leaving me at liberty to smoke like a smudge pot if I chose. But Lloyd scoffed at my father's moldy-fig intransigence on the subject in a way that, on the one hand, verified all my own darkest conclusions, and, on the other, set my teeth on edge. I even took a measure of sly satisfaction in reminding myself that in my dad's private opinion, his brother-in-law was a horse's ass, and that behind Lloyd's back, Dad routinely called him "Void."

I had a pretty good time in DC that summer, pretending to be a responsible, grown-up citizen of the realm. My daily bus commute for work included a brief pause each way in a cavernous, gloomy, subterranean chamber deep in the bowels of the Pentagon (perish the thought), which I figured was probably making me, by osmosis, something of an authority on national defense. And as an embryonic writer (yes, I entertained that fantasy even then), I surely owed it to my future public to get all the worldly experience I could accumulate upon my unsullied—well, slightly sullied—young person, and wasn't I also osmotically soaking up such experience at a prodigious rate just in my daily bus rides through the splendor and squalor of our nation's capital?

The enlightened beings who ran this liberated wet dream of a city had kindly decreed that, at eighteen, I had all the maturity the law required for me to stride into any saloon in town and slap my money down and order up a double zombie if I felt like it. (Yeah, barkeep, and bring it in a dirty glass!) Of course, I didn't even know precisely what a zombie was, and I seriously doubt that I could've survived one anyhow. And besides, at the time, I was happily indulging a youthful infatuation with Miller High Life (once again, I'd fallen for a classy slogan: "The Champagne of Bottled Beer"), and it so happened that on Ninth Street, a short walk from the GAO on the way to my afternoon bus stop, there were bars and beer joints beyond number, in a little skid row outpost tucked away among the gleaming monuments and the official government temples of bureaucratic industry—several unsightly city blocks of shoulder-to-shoulder drinking resorts of very dubious character, along with their attendant SRO hotels, chili parlors, and grind house movie theaters.

It soon became my habit to drop by one or another of the drinking establishments almost every afternoon after work—just to check the quality of their Miller High Life, you understand—and not infrequently to stick around for a couple of chili dogs and an early screening of *Attack of the Cannibal Virgins* or *Hillbilly Jailbait* or *White Trash Nudist Colony*. There was a newsstand on Ninth Street where I'd sometimes pick up a copy of *Police Gazette* to read while I dined, and a Hav-A-Tampa cigar for after. (Hav-A-Tampas came with a wooden tip one could clench in his jaw at a jaunty angle, an ideal prop for my impersonation of a dapper young sport.) Sitting there wreathed in the fumes of a cheap cheroot in some seedy little rathole of a DC bar, fortifying myself for an evening at the theater, an apprentice adult among experts at the work, I endeavored to get acquainted with my new identity. For once in my life, no one was looking over my shoulder, and my anonymity had rendered me barely visible (or so I told myself, although I'm sure the spectacle would've been rewarding for anyone who bothered to look). I was *tabula rasa*, a blank slate, a cipher, an empty vessel filling itself with the Champagne of Bottled Beer.

To an aficionado of adult entertainment such as myself, who had already witnessed the birth of Swedish triplets on the Largest Silver Screen in South-Central Northeastern Kentucky, not to mention having seen with his own two eyes the abundant muchness of Evelyn West and Her Fifty-Thousand-Dollar Treasure Chest—*in person!*—at the Gayety Burlesque Theater in Cincinnati, the Ninth Street movie fare seemed pretty tame, I must say, beguiling titles notwithstanding. Yet I persevered all summer long, coming back whenever the features changed—because, see, you never could tell, the very next minute of whichever execrable film I was subjecting myself to on any given evening might yield up that deliciously sordid scene the lobby posters promised.

(Personally, I would've preferred a bit less titillation, and a lot more … Evelyn West. Nonetheless, even a blind hog finds an acorn now and then, and my persistence was finally rewarded in grand—if unexpected—fashion one evening late that summer, when, in my tireless quest for enlightenment, I happened upon a movie called *Freaks* that left an indelible mark on my consciousness and, eventually, on my writing as well, as though I had dropped a hot coal on my imagination. *Freaks* is a strange, disturbing, morbid monstrosity of a film. It's also a work of pure genius. Don't miss it if you can.)

I even got involved in Washington politics during that momentous summer. Pidge and Lloyd's Parkfairfax apartment was a duplex, currently shared with a newlywed couple, the Wadleighs, the daughter and son-in-law of a sitting US senator from a midwestern state I'll call New Braska (situated somewhere west of New Jersey and east of New Vada). The Wadleighs were subletting their apartment for the summer while the husband, Russell ("Wad," as he was familiarly—and aptly—known), a bumptious, overfed young Alexandria attorney, searched for "more agreeable accommodations."

Senator Virgil Kermode, Mrs. Wadleigh's esteemed papa, had recently distinguished himself by asserting, for public consumption, that Adolf Hitler had personally slipped Joseph Stalin a list of covert homosexuals in the US government so that Stalin could blackmail them and turn them into communist spies. The assertion had been outlandish enough to make the rather obscure senator briefly famous, and the Kermode-Wadleighs basked in the afterglow long after the fire went out. Politically, Pidge and Lloyd were confirmed Democrats, but they too rather enjoyed, thirdhand, the secondhand notoriety of their new acquaintances.

The Wadleighs were often there, having drinks on the patio, when I got in from work. Wad shared Lloyd's enthusiasm for cocktail hour bonhomie, particularly for Lloyd's specialty, his peerless "martoonies"—although Wad insisted they'd be much improved if Lloyd would only add "a wee drop o' Scotch, laddie," to the mix. In my estimation, Wad fully qualified as a horse's ass of Lloydian proportions, albeit of a rather different stripe. Tall and slack-shouldered and pear-shaped, he ornamented the patio like some outsized, ill-conceived work of yard art. He considered himself a great kidder, and he especially liked to tease Pidge about her hillbilly origins (I was beneath Wad's notice, and Lloyd was from Indiana), calling

her Daisy Mae or Mammy Yokum and needling her with half-
assed jokes about Kentucky politics, turning up the volume
on his witless punchlines to make sure everybody got it. ("So,
Daisy Mae, y'know why Mrs. Hadley married Alben Barkley?
She wanted an antique organ! Y'know why Alben Barkley married Mrs. Hadley? *He wanted a used centerpiece!*") Euphonia, the
senator's daughter—named by her politically ambitious parent for the state bird of New Braska—was a stocky but extravagantly shapely onetime high school cheerleader whom Wad,
after a couple of martoonies, liked to tease about the sprinkle
of cinnamon freckles across her pert little nose, insinuating
(or so I supposed) that it constituted some sort of disfiguring
blemish. Privately, I took strong exception to this canard, having personally found Mrs. Wadleigh's freckles quite captivating, a tiny constellation of beauty spots.

Mrs. Wadleigh nee Kermode—Euphonia—was a year or
so nearer my age than she was to her husband's, and she favored girlish fashions like poodle skirts and bobby sox, all of
which helped to justify her spirited presence in my fantasy life
that summer. She and I were on one side of the generational
divide, it seemed to me, and everybody else, certainly including Wad, was on the other. According to my understanding
of the rules in these affairs of the heart, Euphonia and I were
therefore practically secret lovers, a conceit that prompted, in
turn, a full program of highly speculative lubricious scenarios
featuring my improbably cooperative neighbor.

Euphonia, of course, had no interest whatsoever in me,
the geeky, gawky kid from the apartment next door; the interest was all mine—but if prurient interest counts, I had enough

for both of us. Every time she walked across the patio in her white short-shorts—and I must say she inhabited that snug little garment the way nature occupies a vacuum—I heard inside my head the faint strains of that stirring anthem "She's Got Freckles on Her BUT She Is Nice" (my favorite selection on the old Brooksville pool hall jukebox), and my teenage X-ray vision penetrated those short-shorts as if they weren't there, and brought a chimerical second field of freckles into relief so sharp I could've counted them, one by one. "Freckums," her sportive husband called her, in a joshing tone that suggested to my finely tuned ear an enviable familiarity with the (imagined) nether crop. Oh, how I hated him.

"Pidge," the all-too-observant Lloyd announced unceremoniously at breakfast one late-summer Saturday morning, "I do believe old Junior, here,"—that meant me—"has got the red-hots for little Miss Freck." Pidge clucked her tongue at the vulgarity, and then, perhaps to remind me that horse's asses generally ought to be ignored, she suggested that since Lloyd and Wad would be playing golf that afternoon, maybe she and I should take Euphonia roller skating?

Here the attentive reader (are you still there?) may recall my having mentioned, many pages ago, that as an adolescent back in Brooksville, I had become a pretty fair roller skater—good enough, at any rate, that I could still enjoy skating when the opportunity presented itself. And it so happened that on the previous Saturday afternoon, I had discovered a nice rink a short bus ride away in an Alexandria shopping center, and had tried it out, and had come home talking about it.

My skills, I'd found, had not eroded. Afoot, I remained as

disjointedly awkward and uncoordinated as ever—a "sham-
bling, gangling tangle of ganglia," I once described myself—
but put me on skates, friends, and I could move with the
grace and lightness of a swallow on the wing, I could weave
through a crowd of lesser skaters as swiftly and effortlessly
as a passing fancy, I could spin about and skate backwards so
goddamn artistically I sometimes thought I was a figment
of my own imagination. During junior high school, see, I
had been a skate-boy at the Brooksville roller rink, putting
clamp-on skates on girls and younger kids in return for all
the free practice skating I cared to inflict upon myself, plus
tips. Before that, I'd never found even a quasi-athletic pursuit
(dancing very much included, by the way) for which I had the
slightest aptitude, but skating must have liberated my inner
Tinkerbell, for I was soon flitting about the rink like a pixie
on wheels. Once, in a feat of derring-do that stood unmatched
till Evel Knievel began jumping Greyhound buses on his motorcycle, I leapt three Pepsi-Cola cases lined up side by side.
Hey, put me on roller skates and I'd absolutely wow the short-
shorts offa that lady next door!

So, feigning indifference, I accepted Pidge's suggestion
with the standard teenage why-not? shrug (in the dining
room mirror I caught a glimpse of Lloyd smirking behind
his newspaper), and soon the enterprising Pidge was in our
neighbors' kitchen, proposing to drive Euphonia and me to
the rink that afternoon, while the gents went a-golfing. (Pidge
wouldn't be skating herself, she had already told me, but as
an up-to-date, modernistic person, she would enjoy watching
the young people have a good time on their little skates.) Now

Pidge was a very nice aunt, kind and generous to a fault, quite sensible when she hadn't tipped back tee many martoonies—as a secretary, she would've been like Rosalind Russell in *His Girl Friday*, smart and feisty and a bit of a looker—and I'm sure it never crossed her unsuspicious mind that Lloyd was onto something—that, indeed, her owlish nephew was already eyeing the impending occasion as the possible advent of a torrid May-September dalliance, with himself as Mr. May and you-know-who as Mrs. September. As for Wad (Mr. September-to-be), he had apparently signed off on his bride's assignation with his dashing young secret rival (hello!) without a murmur of protest, little suspecting, poor devil, that his happy home was imminently imperiled. So far, so good.

On our way to the skating rink that afternoon, I languished in the back seat of the Buick while Pidge drove (curse you, Lloyd!) and Euphonia cheerfully maligned and reviled the federal government ("… so Daddy says old Truman which as you perhaps know has put this Albert Hiss fella and all these girly-girl pinko comsymps in charge of the henhouse and threw away the keys and …"). In keeping with her avian namesake, Euphonia had a shrill, strident voice with the peculiar property of rendering whatever she was saying instantly irrelevant, like a canary chirping self-importantly in the corner during a noisy cocktail party ("… so Daddy says he ran into old Barkley out in the hall at the United States Senate Office Building which as you perhaps remember Daddy being the well-known United States senator Virgil Kermode and he says Now Alben if you want my opinion you better tell Harry how it seems like in some of these government offices you can't hardly tell the subversives from the homasectuals and Alben which as you perhaps know is the vice president of the United States of America's first name says Well now Virgil ..."). But I was barely listening. As we pulled into the rink's parking lot, I could already hear skate music emanating from within, the recorded pipe organ lustily blasting "Tea for Two" for the listening pleasure of, it seemed, the entire Eastern Seaboard. I strove manfully to maintain a cool exterior; the awaited moment was at hand.

Inside, Euphonia and I rented shoe skates while Pidge settled herself in the spectator section. There were easily a hundred skaters on the floor, many of them little kids buzzing about insanely, like bottle flies with their heads snapped off. The din was tremendous, eight hundred little rock-hard wheels grinding away to the bouncy rhythms of "Rag Mop" on the pipe organ; nonetheless, a few adult-sized couples floated through the chaos as serenely as ballroom dancers, moving to some dreamy rhapsody all their own. Eager to join that happy number, I hurried after Euphonia to a bench on the sidelines and rather grandly flourished a dollar tip at a nearby skate-boy. In an instant the grubby adolescent was kneeling at her feet, lacing her skates for her and trying, as any skate-boy emeritus might've known he would, to look up her poodle skirt. For a fleeting moment I saw through his eyes—such a little pervert that kid was!—and found myself eyeball to eyeball, so to speak, with a pair of dimpled, white, guileless knees, the Honorable Kermode's daughter's disconcerting, mesmerizing knees fairly winking at me! O Muse, where art thou!

Now, while I'm paying off this lecherous little former self

of mine and hurriedly lacing on my own skates, let me explain a thing or three about roller skating: A skilled practitioner of the art such as I was in my prime, you see, powers his forward locomotion by means of long, languorous, balletic strides; he is, at least in his own private movie, a thing of grace and beauty as he glides artfully along. Whereas your rank beginner—Euphonia comes to mind—will spraddle out her skates about a yard apart and stand there teetering helplessly until her youthful yet manly partner—me again—materializes beside her in a masterful Young Lochinvar glissade, catches up her little left hand in his own even as he encircles her waist with his right arm—the brawny arm of a government-certified clerk typist—and, by means of a brief but dazzling display of highly edifying footwork, sweeps her up and sets her in motion and guides her firmly but ever so smoothly into the clockwise flow of passing skaters.

And right there is where (as my friend Wendell likes to say) the bobblin' pin comes off the wobblin' shaft. For at the exact moment that I'm poised on one leg (rather elegantly, if I do say so myself) while I lift my right skate over Euphonia's wandering left skate—which of course has already meandered way the hell over into my personal, private territory—along comes one of those aforementioned pestilential children, some nine-year-old vermin squatting so low over his skates that he's dusting the floor with the seat of his pants, careening around me as heedless as a goddamn bowling ball, and as he passes he clips my weight-bearing skate with a wheel, ever so slightly but just enough to send me pirouetting and pliéing and flailing and floundering ahead in a mortifyingly inartistic fashion, abruptly leaving the fair Euphonia still upright but perilously on her own. Amid my gyrations, I caught a glimpse of her tumbling, ass over teacups as the expression has it, toward the sideline, but by that point it was strictly every man for himself.

Miraculously, I managed to keep my skates under me without going down, but when I finally found my balance and looked behind me, Euphonia was in a heap on the sidelines in front of the spectator section, not far from where we'd started, and that ubiquitous skate-boy was already bending over her, helping her up. To get there, I had to skate all the way around the rink, and by the time I reached them, Euphonia was back on the bench, and Pidge was at her side, mopping her brow with a paper napkin, and the skate-boy was already up to his old tricks, eyeballing those charming knees while he unlaced her skates.

As I came rolling up to them, I heard a familiar, vehemently rancorous voice cry *"Shithead!"* above the ambient racket. Aha! says I to myself, she's caught that sneakin' skate-boy in the act! Shocking epithet, of course, but—and then it dawned on me: Euphonia wasn't addressing the skate-boy. "You little shithead!" she reiterated stoutly, through clenched teeth, presenting her left forearm—which appeared to be intact and, but for a touch of redness at the wrist, unmarked—as though it were some damning piece of evidence against me, a gory bludgeon she'd picked up off the floor. "You made me break my damn arm!"

I did? I glanced at Pidge, who stood, napkin in hand, agape and momentarily frozen in place above the fuming Euphonia. Then she shook her head almost imperceptibly in answer to

my unspoken question, and continued her sympathetic minis-
trations to Euphonia's brow, all the while aiming a distinctly
unsympathetic scowl at the top of Euphonia's oblivious noggin. I knew Pidge well enough to be pretty sure she wasn't
taking umbrage at the unladylike language, so I had to assume (correctly, as things developed) that she'd seen Euphonia come to grief, and understood that this hapless nephew of
hers had been nowhere close to the scene of the crime—which
was gratifying, as far as it went, but in fact the nephew's own
sympathies were actually a good deal more complicated. For
a substantial part of me still yearned to take Euphonia into
my burly clerk-typist arms and comfort her till the cows came
home. Because she really *was* hurt, poor little bird; those were
real tears in her eyes as she inspected her injured forearm,
and she winced when she moved her wrist. And in a way, she
had been right, it really was my fault: When I should've been
holding her up, I'd gotten all preoccupied with saving myself.
I quite agreed that I was a bounder, a varlet, a poltroon—but
"shithead" seemed a little strong.

The skate-boy helped Euphonia get into her saddle shoes,
and Pidge, resolutely solicitous but still unsmiling, led her off
to the ladies' room to try some cold water on her arm. I said
I'd meet them at the car, and turned to cough up yet another
dollar for the skate-boy (speaking of shitheads), who lingered
expectantly.

"Thanks, mister," he said. "Hey, y'know the kid that
tripped you? That was my little brother." Grinning, he pocketed the dollar, and added, "I get him home, I'll kick his ass
for you."

There would be some small satisfaction in that, at least, I told myself glumly on my way to the car; just the prospect of it was a dollar's worth right there—and then too, the promising young chap did call me mister. Moreover, no matter what, there were now two eyewitnesses to my innocence. So why did I still feel guilty?

Pidge and Euphonia came out of the rink a couple of minutes behind me, Euphonia with a damp towel wrapped around her left forearm, still looking, understandably, somewhat peevish. Pidge was all business. There was a hospital in Arlington, she said, and we'd stop at the emergency room on the way home and let somebody take a look at that arm. In the car, Euphonia mercilessly disregarded me all the way; my entire being was apparently as evanescent in her eyes as her short-shorts had been in mine. During the few minutes it took us to get to the hospital, she glared straight ahead and never once looked my way or directed a single word to me. Pidge was uncommonly silent as well, and certainly the much diminished young Mr. Shithead—the former Mr. May—alone and palely loitering in the back seat, had nothing to say for himself. The gloom inside the Buick was so thick it was a wonder Pidge could see to drive.

At the hospital, I waited in the car while Pidge went inside with Euphonia. After a few minutes, I moved up front to the driver's seat, just to remind myself how it felt to sit behind the wheel again. In one more week, my time at GAO would be over, and I'd be back in Maysville, driving my mom's slick new Chevy Bel Air. My pal Ned and I were planning a little field trip into adulthood in the form of a run to Florida in the

Bel Air before we went off to our respective colleges (Ned was the nephew of Pete, my dad's longtime business partner and best friend and—more and more all the time—his drinking buddy), and suddenly I could hardly wait to hit the road. If I'd had Pidge's car keys at that moment, I might've headed straight to Florida all by myself, and left my failed heroics behind in the Arlington hospital emergency room.

I sat there in a stupor of despond for, I guess, half an hour or so until Pidge emerged, alone, from the waiting room. To my surprise, she came straight to the passenger side of the Buick and let herself in.

"Whew, lordy," she said, with a sigh of relief, "that is one aggravatin' young lady. Here,"—she tossed the car keys into my lap—"you drive, hon, let's go home."

Although I'd only driven Lloyd's cherished Buick on that one hair-raising occasion way back in June—and although I knew that to get us home I'd have to negotiate the Parkfairfax exit, the selfsame cloverleaf that had made poor Lloyd scream the loudest—it suddenly seemed perfectly natural to me that I'd be driving us home. It was as if all those back-and-forth miles on the bus had taught me, again through the miracle of osmosis, some nebulous but essential Truth about the very nature of urban automobile traffic itself, and magically rendered me its fearless and intrepid master. Driving that Buick those few minutes turned out to be among the swellest, sweetest rushes I'd ever enjoyed—like learning to walk and learning to swim and learning to skate and learning to ride a bike all rolled up in one glorious moment. And since I'm already preceding my story en route anyhow, I'll just add that this time I drove flawlessly all the way, without incident, terrorizing no one, and navigated even that treacherous cloverleaf as confidently as a sea captain in familiar waters.

But see here, Mr. Shithead (you may well interject, if you've been paying attention), what about poor Euphonia and her broken wing? As I drove, Pidge filled me in: Sure enough, she said, the X-rays showed that Euphonia had a broken arm, a hairline fracture in one of the small bones in her wrist, and right now they were making her a little cast for it. In the meantime, though, she had been emphatically making her presence known throughout the emergency wing of the hospital, informing all the medical personnel within earshot that she was Mizriz Euphonia Wadleigh-knee-Kermode, daughter of *the* Senator Kermode, which, as medical persons theirselfs, they perhaps knew was their steadfast champion in our nation's battle against this old communistical socialized medicine that's about to destroy the very fabric of our society, which as the daughter of a US senator she had the finest hospital insurance the government could buy with our federal tax monies, and was entitled to certain amenities and courtesies, medical-wise, as they perhaps knew.

That said (and a good deal more besides), she had commandeered the receptionist's phone and called Wad—it was late afternoon by now, and the golfers would be home—and told him, still at full volume, how that worthless kid from next door (watch it, lady!) had knocked her off her skates and broke her arm and put her in the hospital, and how Wad was to come and get her right away ("before somebody shoots her," Pidge added, under her breath); but first he was to pack them a bag, because they were going straight from the hospital to Daddy's nice suite at the Mayflower Hotel for the duration of her recovery, which was going to take quite a while if she had anything to say about it.

I didn't know it then, of course, but I would ne'er see Euphonia more, alas. The Mayflower must have proved an agreeable asylum, for the Wadleighs never returned. One afternoon a few days later, according to the Parkfairfax super, Wad came by, alone, and picked up their belongings, and by the time Pidge and Lloyd and I got home from work that day, Wad and Euphonia Wadleigh, knee Kermode, were but a memory.

As for that rueful "alas," however, I just threw that in for poetic effect; actually, short of shooting her myself, I was quite prepared to dismiss the lady from my thoughts at the earliest opportunity. Pidge indicated that she too had enjoyed a sufficiency of Euphonia Wadleigh, thank you very much, and was ready to go home and get busy on her Saturday afternoon cocktails. At least that silly Wad won't be hanging around, she said, him and his stupid hillbilly jokes—Pidge was pretty sure she'd seen his car back there in the cloverleaf, headed the other way—so we could finally have a nice, peaceful evening on the patio for a change.

Which we did. It was martoonie time, and Lloyd was there to greet Pidge with a tall pitcher of the celebrated elixir when we pulled into the driveway. I feared the worst when he saw me get out of his Buick on the driver's side, but he never said a word about it. Instead, he just told me there was a six-pack in the fridge, and to refresh myself accordingly. (It was

Miller's, for which I'd recently confessed a special fondness.) Then Pidge recounted our misadventures for him, mercifully omitting, with a sly wink in my direction, Euphonia's unflattering assessment of my character, in light of the certainty that Lloyd (as she and I both knew) would surely have found the sobriquet "shithead," as applied to her favorite (and only) nephew, all too irresistible.

But Lloyd got an otherwise full account of Euphonia's emergency room soliloquy, including how she'd tried to blame me for the calamity even though I had nothing— nothing much—to do with it. And besides, Pidge said, she was fed up to here with the way these Wadleighs and that old Senator Commode were always throwing off on decent public servants like, well, like your Uncle Lloyd here, for instance, calling them sissies and all. ("Sissies?" Lloyd said, looking up quickly, as though he hadn't thought of it that way before.) So she and Euphonia weren't on real good terms when they parted, and Pidge had a notion we wouldn't be seeing much of the Wadleighs from here on out. Lloyd, in turn, said he'd caught Wad kicking his ball out of the rough three different times that afternoon when he thought Lloyd wasn't watching, and therefore it wouldn't break Lloyd's heart if he never laid eyes on another New Braskan for the remainder of his natural life.

In tribute to that happy prospect, Lloyd raised his martoonie glass, treated himself to a long, audible sip, smacked his lips in satisfaction, and added, scornfully, "Wee drop o' Scotch my ass." And that—Lloyd's ass—was basically our final word regarding the Commode-Wadleighs before they were swallowed whole—and not a minute too soon—down the bottomless gullet of history.

—

On the following Friday evening, after my last day at GAO, I took the overnight train home to Maysville, and a couple of days later, Ned and I lit out in that fine canary-yellow-and-charcoal-gray Bel Air for the sunny sands of Florida, where we frolicked away the end of our extended adolescence as if there were no tomorrow—but this time I'll spare you the details. Suffice it to say that we topped off our summer in high style, preparing ourselves for the rigors of higher education by soaking our intellects in beer, to condition them for the life of the mind.

Thus prepared, early on a September Monday morning, I am crossing the Ohio River from Maysville on the Simon Kenton Bridge, traveling with my parents in the latest edition of my dad's green Pontiac sedan. The day is still in its infancy, the morning sun just topping the Kentucky hills behind us, shreds of mist still rising from the surface of the river. My mom is in the backseat, my dad, uncharacteristically, is riding shotgun (he has a hangover), and I, to my own surprise, am at the wheel. (My dad doesn't ordinarily like being a passenger in his own car, so this hangover must be especially nettlesome.) We are bound for the ivied halls of Spoonbred U, an eight- or nine-hour drive southeast into the dark recesses of the heart of Dixie, where, first thing tomorrow morning, I am to begin participating in a mysterious, vaguely creepy-sounding ritual called Freshman Orientation, and if I survive three days of that ordeal—which I will—I'll set forth the next day on what is destined to become forty peripatetic years of wandering the trackless groves of academe. My fate is sealed.

But all of that awaits me in a future I haven't even begun to imagine yet. Right now, I'm piloting that big green boxcar of a Pontiac across the bridge, and the only future that interests me starts and ends with the pack of Luckies in my shirt pocket. Although I've been visibly—yea, brazenly—carrying cigarettes on or about my person ever since I got back from Washington almost three weeks ago, trailing my spoor behind me in overflowing ashtrays all over the house, I still haven't ventured to light up in my father's presence. Today, we've been up since daybreak, bolting breakfast, loading suitcases in the car (my suitcases, mostly; my parents will be back home tomorrow evening), with not a single opportunity to sneak off for a few quick drags; and now, as we approach the stop sign at the end of the bridge, I am flat perishing for a smoke.

Meanwhile, my dad, being under no such constraint, is even at this very moment applying his trusty Zippo to what is probably already his fourth or fifth Viceroy of the morning. (He has recently switched to filter tips, for their healthful properties.) He takes a long, salutary drag, clicks the Zippo shut, and exhales a blooming cloud of good, wholesome tobacco smoke, thoroughly filtered of all impurities. I am consumed with envy; I *have* to have a cigarette. At the stop sign, having gathered up, out of a mélange of desperation, timorousness, and bravado, every scrap of self-respect I can muster,

I fish a Lucky from my shirt pocket, hang it—nonchalantly, I hope—on my lip, and turn to my father for a light.

He cocks his handsome left eyebrow at me and smiles ever so slightly, a look of mildly amused skepticism that I'm all too familiar with, having known it all my life. To me it always means something like: *Am I supposed to take you seriously?* He moves as if to pass me his lighter, but before I can take it from him, he snaps his fingers, the Zippo's lid obediently flips itself open, the familiar blue flame leaps from his thumbnail to the tip of my cigarette.

"You're the driver," he says. "So drive."

VII. The Apparel Oft Proclaims the Man

That attentive reader I've been so optimistically invoking will hardly be surprised to learn that Spoonbred U did not succeed in transmogrifying me into a Southern Gentleman. As noted, I already had my doubts about the hallowed Honor System—it certainly hadn't worked on me!—and they were all confirmed when I realized that the whole system depended on everybody's readiness to rat out everybody else. This revealed itself to me when, only a month or so into our first semester, one of my new friends got turned in to the Honormeisters by a friend of *his* for refusing to turn in a friend of *theirs*, a guy he *thought* he'd seen stealing glimpses of what *might* have been a cheat-sheet, during a geology quiz. A den of snitches! General Spoonbred's Finishing School for Southern Gentlemen, where we learn to spy on each other like a bunch of Rooskies! Shades of Senator Commode!

Any illusions I may have entertained about the spiritual rewards of higher education were dashed when one of my freshmen classmates—a soft-spoken boy named Walter, from, fittingly, Paine City, Tennessee—despondent because he'd been rejected by his father's fraternity, barricaded himself in his dorm room one Saturday night while the rest of us were out getting hammered at our respective frat houses, and shot himself to death with a German Luger, a trophy his star-crossed father had brought home from the War. I was beginning to entertain some serious second thoughts about this place.

The eight or nine hundred young Johnny Rebs who comprised the undergraduate Spoonbred student body were (at least in their sober moments) perhaps the most conventional, hidebound, unimaginative band of rebels ever assembled. They seemed almost unanimously to aspire to become alcoholic small-town attorneys. There was a strictly enforced campus dress code—coat and tie at all times—which meant, as per *la mode du jour* for Southern Gentlemen, classrooms and hallways clotted with seersucker (in cool weather, charcoal-gray flannel), rep striped neckties, and oxford cloth button-downs wherever one looked, the whole tableau sprinkled with freshman beanies, idiotic little Spoonbred-gold skullcaps that made the wearer question the current status of his own manhood; while virtually every foot that trod the World's Longest Concrete Footbridge was shod in highly burnished brown cordovan. The middle-aged young men of Spoonbred were on the march!

Which reminds me: At the very top of my list of grievances was ROTC—or, as it was appropriately pronounced,
Rotsie. The Korean conflict was in full swing by then, and
the specter of the military draft loomed ominously over every able-bodied young male in the land, myself among them.
Small schools like Spoonbred were hastily contriving to tack
a military program on to their curriculum, in their patriotic
quest to become safe havens for draft-averse slackers like me.
Spoonbred had landed an army program, but because it was
brand new, the only guys on hand with any prior experience
were those who'd gone to a military high school—which is
to say the ones who'd been *sent off* to military school, usually because their families couldn't stand having them around
the house another minute. And those guys—who tended to
be, not to put too fine a point upon it, the most insufferable,
overbearing, egregiously detestable Southern Gentlemen
on campus—were installed as the student officers in our
wretched little army of the unwilling. Suddenly, that mouthy
little whistledick who lived down the hall in the dorm, and
who had already earned my eternal enmity by correcting my
pronunciation in French class, became Lieutenant Whistledick, my platoon leader!

On Saturday mornings, we donned our government-
issue, war surplus, olive-drab dress uniforms—itchy, ill-fitting
suits of woolen armor the thickness of a horse blanket, jack-
boots that always felt like they were on the wrong feet—for
three delightful hours of close-order drill. I hated close-order
drill above all other human activity. To the surprise of no girl
or woman who has ever survived the enlightening ordeal of

dancing with me, I'm constitutionally incapable of keeping a beat, either on the dance floor or, as I soon discovered, on the drill field. (Now if we'd drilled on roller skates, I coulda showed 'em a thing or two.) It was my fate to be forever out of step with my fellow man—which of course I already knew, in the metaphorical sense, but here was undeniable, empirical evidence to confirm it. No matter how rigorously I counted cadence in my head, my feet marched to—what else?—a different drummer, one with a bad case of Caucasian arrhythmia. These people simply could not stay in step with me! My superior officer, Lt. Whistledick—real name Maynard Balch, of Yazoo City, Mississippi—whose bane I surely was (as he was most surely mine), helpfully suggested that I put a sharp rock in my right boot—a very sharp rock—to remind me which foot was which. I tried a penny, but it didn't work. It was manifestly clear (at least to me, if not so much to the unwitting objects of my attentions) that I was meant to be a lover, not a fighter.

On the plus side, unlike poor Walter, I was deemed acceptable by the fraternity my dad had been in long ago, during his one year at UK. Social life at Spoonbred was nonexistent outside the frat houses, so joining seemed by far the most agreeable expedient open to me at the moment: an easy way to get into a fairly well-regarded fraternity without much risk of rejection (Walter's unfortunate experience notwithstanding), and at the same time to ingratiate myself with my father at no cost whatsoever to my own inflated self-esteem. But then, early in the second semester, my new brotherhood held an initiation ceremony for neophyte members, and I heard myself take a solemn oath that, on pain of immediate and perpetual expulsion from the fraternal bosom, I would never knowingly allow any person of African or Hebrew descent to pollute the rolls of Sigma Omicron Bubba, thereby to besmirch the honor of all SOBs throughout history.

I took the pledge, but I had private reservations. At Spoonbred, we were always pledging this or that: "I pledge I have neither given nor received aid on this quiz/exam/term paper," etc., etc.—so many pledges, indeed, that the words were already losing their meaning, as the gloss of sincerity wore away. There was something about this one, though, that left an unpleasant aftertaste. In childhood, I'd been encouraged by my ex-schoolteacher mom and her several schoolteacher sisters to develop an appetite for reading, with one result being that by ten or eleven, I'd read both *Uncle Tom's Cabin* and *The Adventures of Huckleberry Finn*—and just as their authors cunningly intended, those seditious works had made a juvenile closet liberal out of me. I didn't actually know any Hebrews or Africans on a personal level, but I was all in with Nigger Jim and Uncle Tom and Topsy and them. If it was up to me, I'd have made them all honorary posthumous SOBs, Topsy included.

I realized, though, that these sentiments would not have endeared me to the brethren, and had perhaps best be kept under my freshman beanie. Yet they were an irksome presence in my thoughts, a nagging reminder that my friend Ned's college—Miami of Ohio—was reputed to be, at least by comparison, a shining bastion of civil liberty and racial tolerance. Never mind that Miami's athletic teams called themselves the

Redskins, or that there were probably fewer than a hundred blacks in the entire five thousand–strong student body; it was the thought that counted.

In my first semester at Spoonbred, I had distinguished myself academically by racking up a string of perfectly matched C-minuses, and as the second semester dragged along, I didn't see much reason to hope for improvement—and I suppose I should congratulate myself for my prescience, because I ended that semester with a complete matched set of C-minuses, an unblemished record of mediocrity. When it comes to mediocrity, you can't beat a C-minus.

Nor was my romantic life thriving. On most weekends the fraternity would either import a bevy of blind dates from one of the several women's colleges in our orbit—Randolph-Macon or Sweet Briar or Mary Baldwin or Hollins—or some of the older brothers with cars would assemble a blind-date foray (a pussy posse, in Spoonbred parlance) to a dance at one or another of those citadels of feminine virtue, but for me, these ventures were foredoomed. I had convinced myself somehow that becoming a college man would automatically make a better dancer of me, and when that didn't work, I was, in the popular circumlocution of the day, s.o.l. I still went through the motions (so to speak), still walked unsuspecting blind dates onto the dance floor and trudged around with them in a forced march through a few slow numbers, but it was uphill work all the way. Naturally, I couldn't talk and dance at the same time ("multitasking" hadn't even been invented yet), so as a rule my dates and I remained perfect strangers. No doubt my dancing gave each of those persevering young ladies plenty to remember me by, but of the dozen or so blind dates I took dancing that year, I remember only one: a tall, lanky girl from Alabama who must've had singularly large feet, because I kept stepping on them all evening.

Meanwhile, my thoughts drifted inexorably northward, in the general direction of Miami of Ohio, where girls of every description ran as wild and naked as tree frogs, where the races melded like coffee and cream, and society had evolved to such an extent that they sold beer to eighteen-year-olds! Miami, where there was no Sigma Omicron Bubba chapter (thanks to that "African or Hebrew descent" clause in the vows), so that one could disdain fraternities even while flaunting one's own fraternity pin (I actually did this), to assure that no one mistook him for a reject. Miami, where, according to Ned, you could take a whole class in something called "creative" writing, which I thought might help me raise that C-minus average a notch or two. (By the way, it worked perfectly: a year later, the first story I submitted as a rookie in that very writing class would pull in ... a C-plus!) There was no dress code at Miami, hence a person was free to express his own basic personal goddamn individuality, if he had any left after a couple of terms at Spoonbred. I'd still have to take ROTC, of course—they didn't give draft deferments for incompetent marching—but at least I could leave Lt. Whistledick back at Spoonbred to defend Western Civilization's southern flank. As for me, it was time I took command of my own destiny. By spring break, I had made up my mind: next fall, I promised myself, I was transferring to Miami.

My dad was not going to be thrilled with this scheme.

He had rather enjoyed having an embryonic Southern Gent in the family, and presumably would have been content to watch the little fellow grow into a small-town lawyer, even an alcoholic one—or better yet, a rising junior executive (quite certainly an alcoholic one) in the Triangle Towing Company. And I knew he'd been pleased that I had chosen—and been chosen by—his old fraternity, even though he never said a word about it, before or after. (It would take me a lot of years of reflection to realize what a kindness that was.) Anyhow, disclosing my plan was a daunting prospect, and I went home for spring vacation week filled with an untenable admixture of resolve and dread. But there was no getting 'round it, he must be told, and it was up to me and me alone to grasp the bull manfully by the short hairs and step up to the plate and take a deep breath and haul off and ... and try to get my mom to break the news.

My strategy was simply to play that creative writing course at Miami like a Stradivarius. To that purpose, what had been just an enticing future career option needed to become, overnight, a full-blown calling. I had heard (I would explain to my sweet, forbearing mom) the siren song of the muse (or words to that effect), and I must answer the call! Next fall, I must hie me thither to Miami, where I can learn the tricks of the creative writing trade and become a certified—yes!—an official, certified "Freelance Writer!" (That job description had always had, for me, a jaunty, adventurous character, and I supposed it would probably be an easy line of work, once a person got the hang of it.) Anyhow, I figured I could make a fairly compelling case for myself, and that I'd soon have my mom persuaded that she too could hear some faint echo of my muse's clarion call.

Throughout my waking life my mother had negotiated the breach between my dad and me, holding us at bay from each other as a means of keeping us together. She was a born politician, my mom was, although she never ran for anything; but people liked her in the way they like the all-too-rare incorruptible public servant. (She came by the talent honestly, inasmuch as the Poages of Brooksville were a political family, with a long history in local public service. My great grandfather had been elected circuit court clerk of Bracken County around 1880, and had been succeeded by my grandfather, who was succeeded in turn by my Aunt Lutie. Among the three of them, they held that modest but useful office for almost eighty years.)

My mother, Jessie, had other gifts as well: She had a genius for management, for running a tight ship, for putting things in order and keeping them there, and she was a self-taught but flawless bookkeeper—skills that made her indispensable to the Triangle Towing Company, which she served officially as secretary/treasurer and, unofficially, as an in-house source of wisdom, a common-sense counterweight to my dad's vaulting ambition. Unfailingly pleasant and good-natured, she nonetheless had a low tolerance for foolishness, and a disarming way of cutting directly to the heart of the matter. She was a terrific cook, a meticulous housekeeper, a gracious hostess, and—I'm here to tell you—an affectionate, attentive mother. A natural athlete, she'd been a high school basketball star; later in her life, she became an accomplished horsewoman. On top of all that, she was radiantly pretty; when I was eight or nine, and *The Wizard of Oz* finally made its way to Brooksville, I thought Glinda the Good Witch looked exactly like my mom, only not as pretty—and, for that matter, not as Good either.

(My mother's forthrightness was another heirloom Poage family characteristic, this one handed down to her by her own mother, Gertrude Poage—"Miss Gert," as just about everyone called her—a formidable, no-nonsense matriarch, much loved and widely revered. Once, when I was in high school, I was dispatched to Brooksville on election day, to drive her to the polls at the county courthouse. Afterward, as we were making our way back to the car, I asked, rather breezily, "Well, Miss Gert, how'd you vote?" Her reply was instantaneous, and chastening. "With a pencil!" she snapped.)

Of course a paragon of a mother such as mine would defend her cub, and I had come to understand that, privately, my mom was often on my side when my dad and I had differences. But there was yet another bond between us, an affinity which, when I stumbled upon it, had taken me completely by surprise:

For my father was, at heart, a Johnsville boy, and when he married a Brooksville girl, he brought a few Johnsville attitudes to town with him. In Johnsville, a girl who smoked would've been viewed with grave suspicion by local society, and my father was of the same opinion; if my mother had been inclined to smoke, she would've been subject to the same strictures I'd found so oppressive. Although young ladies in cosmopolitan Brooksville were generally of a more adventurous stamp—"more modernistic," as my Aunt Pidge (who, in her time, had been one of them) would have put it—to my knowledge, my mother had never taken even one tiny puff.

Now imagine my astonishment when, one afternoon near the end of my senior year of high school, I came home to an empty house, famished as usual, and, with my mind's eye fixed on the cold pot roast left over from last night's dinner, went straight to the kitchen stove and flung open the oven door and found ... a cigarette! With lipstick on it! There it was, a solitary cigarette, white as a piece of chalk in the darkened oven, lying on the metal rack right in front of the pot roast platter, an entire Viceroy with my mother's shade of lipstick on the cork-tipped end and a short ash on the other, not stubbed out but abandoned in haste, left there to expire on its own.

I closed the oven door feeling vaguely embarrassed, as though I'd inadvertently wandered into someone else's house—sort of like the feeling I'd had when I discovered that my dad was in cahoots with a condom dealer. There could be only one scenario here: My mom—a secret smoker, just like me!—had boosted a smoke from my dad, and had been copping a quick one in the kitchen when she heard him coming her way, and had coolly popped the evidence into the oven. (Quick thinking, Mom! Thirty-six years later, when I am getting busted for possession and unaccountably fail to eat the evidence—a teensy morsel of a roach!—I will regret that I didn't inherit your presence of mind.) There was even a spent match on the stovetop, corroborating the obvious: I had a co-conspirator, a silent partner in crime.

As I was leaving the kitchen, it occurred to me that my dad also sometimes had an afternoon appetite for cold roast beef—so, on a sudden inspiration, I went back to the stove and grabbed the cigarette and the burnt match and chucked them in the wastebasket. A few minutes later, I was sitting in the living room when my parents came in the front door. My dad sat down to read the afternoon paper, while my mom went directly to the kitchen—and the stove. I heard her open the oven, close it, then quickly open it again, as if to confirm what she'd seen there—or, more precisely, what she hadn't seen. Afterward, during supper, I saw her glance quizzically at me a time or two, but we never exchanged a word about it, neither that evening nor ever after. Yet it remained in place between us, an unspoken word, a solemn bond: trust.

Sometime during my first few months at Spoonbred, my mother had apparently also called my father's bluff; for when I came home for Christmas vacation, she too had begun smoking determinedly (perhaps even a bit defiantly) in my father's presence. I asked her about it, and she said that at first he'd raised a real hee-cack (her all-purpose word for any sort of ruckus), but she told him she was sick and tired of all the fuss on that subject in her house, and she didn't want to hear another word about it.

So I understood that I could count her as an ally, and at spring break, I came home loaded for bear with reasons why I needed to transfer to Miami at the soonest opportunity. Even so, I kept that plan under wraps for the first couple of days, biding my time; with patience as my watchword, I awaited the right moment to disclose my true intentions. ("Whenever they get his chickenshit up," a long-ago drinking associate once sang of me, to the tune of "Clancy Lowered the Boom,"

"McClanahan leaves the room-room-room …") Meanwhile, I used the interim to deride and disparage, in a generic whine that pretty thoroughly permeated the entire household, all things Spoonbred, right down to its chronically inept football team—although the only game I'd actually attended all season was on one of those fraternity-orchestrated blind dates, this one with a burly Sweet Briar sophomore who could probably have made linebacker on either squad.

On my third morning at home, I slept in, after an evening of convivial debauchery with a few scapegrace old Maysville High acquaintances of mine. By the time I finally bestirred myself the next morning, my dad had long since left the house, so, finding my mom sitting alone in the kitchen, smoking her morning Parliament ("Tobacco Tastes Best When the Filter's Recessed!"), I knew I had to make my move. I mooched a Parliament, tore off the weird little tubular blowgun of a filter, lit up, survived a brief coughing fit (unfiltered, it was like smoking a hairball), and endeavored to ease into the subject of my future by means of a little additional all-purpose grousing about how Spoonbred was so stuffy and old-timey and "anti-deluvian" (an impressive new word I'd recently mislearned in Ancient History class) that it didn't even offer any modern, up-to-date courses in, like, say, freelance writing, fer crissakes …

"Well," she interrupted me to say, "your father thinks you better transfer to Miami."

He does? I couldn't have been more surprised if she'd said my father had told her to give me two dollars for that nice lady down on Front Street.

"He thinks you're about to flunk out of school," she went on. "He says that's why you're doing so much griping about it. You better go someplace easier, he says."

Whoa! My first impulse was to take umbrage and fly into high dudgeon, from which vantage point I could sputter some appropriately indignant response. True, I wasn't exactly setting the Rappahannock afire at Spoonbred, but I certainly wasn't flunking out. Those C-minuses might not be golden, but at least they were fungible; I could cash 'em in at any not-too-choosy institution of my choosing. On the other hand, however, I had but to accept my father's insultingly lowball assessment of my capacities and prospects, and—hot damn!—come next fall, I'd be Miami-bound!

Okay, I decided on the spot, I can live with that. Hell yeah, "Opprobrium" is my middle name! Ignominy is destiny! Onward to Miami!

"Well," my mother said, "you might have a higher opinion of yourself if you'd get those grades up."

No argument there; better grades would undoubtedly do wonders for my self-esteem. But if I'd learned anything at all in my time at Spoonbred, it was that, as a scholar, I had certain limitations, and I didn't foresee much likelihood that I'd be overcoming them any time soon. Fortunately (as I patiently explained to my beloved but benighted mom), we blithe spirits in the freelance writing game weren't obliged to be scholars; we had only to lollygag around accumulating great, sticky gobs of Real Life Experience all over ourselves, the raw material from which we spin those captivating tales of our adventures.

Okay, try selling *your* mom on a career plan like that; she wouldn't buy it, I'll bet, and mine wouldn't either. "You just better get to work on those grades, buster," she warned again, stabbing out her Parliament as she rose to go. "Alma Potts will stick your fanny in the army before you know it."

Now there, friends, was a sobering thought. Miss Alma Potts was the clerk of the Mason County Draft Board. A tiny wisp of a maiden lady, Miss Potts was believed, among draft-eligible Maysville youth, to wield enormous, generally malign influence over the diabolical proceedings of the all-powerful draft board, and was known to look with special loathing upon college guys who got nice, comfortable deferments and then didn't keep their grades up.

Left alone to smoke the remains of my de-filtered gasper (it tasted awful, but I didn't want to waste it), I contemplated my mom's dire parting admonition. Rotsie, bless its wizened little heart, would keep me draft-proof through a sophomore year at Miami, but … then what? Dast I hope creative writing would pull me through? Yes! With my stern, unforgiving muse Miss Alma Potts riding my shoulder like a succubus, urging me ever onward, yes, I dast! Of course those C-minuses at Spoonbred were, for all practical purposes, already writ in stone; no last-minute surge of brainpower (not that I could've generated one) was going to improve them or erase them. But in light of these new developments, I needn't start worrying about any of that, I figured, till around this time next year, and by then, what the hey, I'd probably have my first novel finished.

Greatly heartened by that jolly prospect, I turned my

attention to the more immediate future. With only a couple of months left at Spoonbred, I needed to think about how best to tell that temple of intransigence it could kiss its anti-bellum ass good-bye for me. I entertained a mean, niggling little impulse to administer some sort of small comeuppance to the place before I left it, to burn a bridge or two, but (aside from torching the World's Longest Concrete Footbridge), so far, nothing had occurred to me.

I was still pondering the matter on the following Sunday evening, when I was to take the overnight train back to school. The train, I knew from experience after Thanksgiving break and Christmas vacation, would be picking up fellow collegians heading back to their respective schools at every stop—Ashland, Huntington, Charleston, points south—most of them determined to wring the last inebrious drop of pleasure out of spring break, and as our numbers grew and merriment prevailed, many a flagon of cheap grog would make the rounds while we rolled on through the night, deep into the land of doo-wah-diddie. (I'd already laid by a pint of hundred-proof Old Tub as my share of the provisions.) Early Monday morning I and about a dozen Spoonbrethren would woozily detrain and straightway pile into one of several waiting taxis with as many other hungover Spoonboobs as the cab would accommodate and dash across town to the campus, arriving in the skimpiest nick of time to dump our suitcases at the dorm and high-tail it to an eight o'clock class—in my case, Military Science & Tactics, the classroom portion of ROTC, wherein we were learning, among other military secrets, how to distinguish between trench foot and trench mouth. (No, the sergeant who taught the class wearily acknowledged in response to a student's question, you don't get trench mouth from sucking your toes.) Uniforms weren't required in the Rotsie classroom, but the campus dress code applied as usual. Late arrivals would be subject to innumerable extra hours on the drill field; AWOLs would be slapped with an instant dishonorable discharge from ROTC—which, paradoxically, would render them readily available for the military draft.

Now after all those months at Spoonbred, I was terminally weary of the oppressive sameness imposed by that accursed campus dress code; coats and ties and cordovan shoes had become sackcloth and ashes to me. So I had come home without any of those trappings, knowing that when it was time to return, I could piece together enough leftover high school odds and ends to pass inspection by the campus apparel police, whose prying eyes, thanks to the ubiquitous Honor System, were—quite literally—everywhere. I would wear clothes for which I'd long since lost any trace of affection, and after wallowing around in them all night on the train, I could go directly to class right out of the taxi, rumpled and pungent but nonetheless in full compliance, technically if not aesthetically, with the dress code.

In the furthermost corner of my closet, I located a coat I'd owned since early high school, the very first article of clothing I had ever chosen for myself and bought with my own money—money I'd earned by the sweat of my brow, jerking soda at Kilgus's Drugstore—a boxy, powder-blue sport coat with zoot suit shoulder pads the size of bricks, and royal-blue spread-wing lapels and matching patch pockets that hung at my sides like saddlebags. As you might imagine, my dad loathed this festive garment to the very core of his being, which of course is what I considered its best feature. Later, I had even scored a pair of blue suede Thom McAns to go with it—and when I came across those too in the back of the closet, I thought okay, somebody's trying to tell me something. So I dragged them out as well—real urban clodhopppers they were, with crepe soles an inch and a half thick—and they reminded me that the high-waisted navy-blue corduroys I used to wear with them were right where they'd been for the last two years, at the bottom of the bottom drawer of my dresser. Out they came, a couple of inches too short but as ruggedly imperishable as ever. Finally, to accessorize my burgeoning ensemble, I found an extra-wide, hand-painted necktie—what Tom Wolfe, himself a Spoonbred alum, would've called a "big lunch" tie—a Christmas gift from my ninth-grade girlfriend, depicting an autumn scene replete with falling leaves, pumpkins, a Thanksgiving turkey, even a troupe of tiny square dancers gamboling merrily beneath a harvest moon, all rendered in lurid living color.

Thus equipped, I stepped into the high-waisted high-water corduroys and laced on my blue suede roach-stompers, looped the autumnal cravat around my neck and tied it in a full Windsor knot as big as my fist, donned my decorative blue vestment, slipped the pint of Old Tub into one of my voluminous patch pockets, and checked myself out in the mirror on the closet door. To my dubious credit, I immediately recognized the comedic potential of these clownish duds—in that two-tone blue livery with the brick shoulder pads, I might've been mistaken for a doorman, or a drum major in a marching band, or a 1950s-vintage airline stewardess; whereas the blue suede clodhoppers bespoke Li'l Abner on a Saturday night— yet I really liked the singularity of it all, the very fact that, for once, I'd be the only person at Spoonbred who didn't look like everybody else at Spoonbred. At least for one brief moment in time, I could thumb my nose at sartorial tyranny—a hollow victory at best, since probably no one would even notice, but what the hell, it was a start.

On the train, the party-minded among us soon found each other and eventually commandeered one end of a passenger car, and composed ourselves for a long, bibulous night. My regalia was good for a few chuckles, and late in the proceedings I and a couple of other convivial art aficionados lifted a dollop of Old Tub in tribute to the anonymous genius who hand-painted the masterpiece on my necktie. On Monday morning the train arrived on schedule, the taxis were waiting, and I landed on campus dressed for class, which afforded me enough spare time to grab a cup of coffee and a doughnut before ROTC. It wasn't unusual for guys to show up on the first morning after a break looking somewhat seedier than your ordinary everyday Southern Gentleman, and nobody gave me a second glance in Rotsie class. Later that morning, I had a break between classes, time enough to hustle over to the dorm and slip into something less confrontational. But no one else seemed to be paying much attention to their (or my) attire that morning, so I opted instead to administer another dose of coffee to myself and give my full attention to my hangover. That kept me awake long enough to make it

to another class, which I slept through, and then another ...
which I slept through. I ate lunch enveloped in a fog so dense
that it obscured whatever unidentified substance I was eating,
and then, still in a semi-comatose condition, I somehow found
my way to a two-hour geology lecture ... which, you may be
sure, I slept through.

By the time I finally made it to the dorm, I found that my
roommate, a bright-eyed, hard-nosed little wise guy named
Richard, from Danbury, Connecticut, had already reinstalled
himself in our cramped two-man ensquatment, and was at his
desk, studying industriously.

"Hey, Clammerham," he said, without looking up, when I
came in. "Take your hat and jacket off."

Richard was one of the very few blessings Spoonbred
had bestowed upon me: a compatible roommate. Unlike me
or the vast majority of our classmates, Richard didn't come
from "people of means"; his father, the paterfamilias of a large
Catholic family, was a linotype operator at the local newspaper, and Richard was at Spoonbred by the grace of some
kind of needs-based government scholarship that kept him on
short rations, and obliged him to bus tables and wash dishes
in the campus cafeteria for pocket money and leftovers. He
was a smart, lively, attractive guy, and several fraternities had
wasted complimentary meals, invitations to parties, and the
like, trying to recruit him, even though he didn't have the
preferred southern-fried pedigree. He cheerfully accepted
their attentions and emoluments, while rejecting their entreaties out of hand, pleading poverty. I was a year older and
half a head taller than Richard, but he had, at eighteen, about

twenty years of maturity on me. He was no deep thinker, but he compensated with a sort of shrewdness that was almost better than wisdom, and what he lacked in brilliance he made up for in diligence. A natural-born skeptic and smart aleck (that crack about the hat and jacket would stay with me until I put it in my novel, thirty years later), Richard looked with wry incredulity upon all the antebellum ancestor worship that smothered Spoonbred like gravy on a pork chop.

"Damn!" he said, when he caught sight of the jacket I was actually wearing at the moment. "Did you mug a scarecrow? They catch you on the campus in that outfit, bud, they'll ship your hillbilly ass straight to Andersonville."

They'd better hurry, then, I told him, because in two more months I'd be long gone. This was no surprise to Richard, of course; after months of back-to-back confinement in that wretched little cell, he and I didn't have many secrets between us. Like me, Richard was scheming to part company with Spoonbred; he was hoping that, after this semester, the government would see fit to let him take his scholarship home to Connecticut, where his high school sweetheart was languishing impatiently at the state university.

Indeed, Richard and I had even confided certain heretical misgivings as to the sacred honor code, and had agreed that it could be much improved by a few minor situational adjustments, which we were prepared to undertake, albeit surreptitiously and anonymously. Consider, for instance, those accursed reading pledges we signed for freshman English every Friday, solemnly attesting that we had frittered away six hours of our precious leisure time during the past week poring over some slouchy old mudpuppy like, say, *Moby Dick*. Yeah, right. As we understood it, forty-five minutes of *Moby Dick* uses up at least six hours off the far end of a person's life expectancy. We had our own honor system, me and Richard: He didn't keep a time card on me, and I honored his confidence by not keeping one on him. As far as Richard was concerned, it was all part of being a good Catholic; do unto others, and so forth. But to hint aloud at such bald-faced apostasy on the Spoonbred campus would put one at risk of being taken for a Hostile, and shot on sight; therefore we kept our counsel, and conspired by winks and nods to cheat the clock on a weekly basis.

So while I re-insinuated myself into my half of our meager accommodation, I told Richard how the sheer eloquence of my reasoning (yeah, right) had persuaded my parents to approve the transfer to Miami, and Richard told me, in turn, that the government had succumbed to his entreaties, and that he'd be transferring too. After we'd congratulated each other on our forthcoming liberation, he asked me about the provenance of my interesting new wardrobe, of which I happened to be partially divesting my aromatic self at that very moment, in preparation for a much-needed sponge bath. (For all our preppy, high-end togs, we Spoonbred princelings didn't trouble ourselves overmuch with weekday showers, there being no delicate female sensibilities on the premises.) I admitted that I'd painstakingly selected each article for its exceptional unsightliness, in the interest of making myself a walking eyesore to the greater glory of Spoonbred U, and Richard said, Well, in that case, it was a big success. I went off to wash up, and by the time I got back to the room, it was getting on toward time for Richard to punch in at the cafeteria for the early-evening shift. I'd be leaving soon, as well, for dinner at the SOB house— coat and tie compulsory—presenting a dilemma that Richard paused long enough to frame before he left.

"You wearing that hayseed outfit to dinner?" he asked. I admitted I was thinking about it. "You should just wear that all the time from now on," he said, laughing, as he went out. "Give your fratboys something to remember you by."

After he was gone, I *did* think about it, at least momentarily. I had crossed paths on the campus that day with a number of Sigma Omicron Bubbas, and a few had smirked or otherwise looked askance, but mostly they were too preoccupied with their own post-vacation hangovers to care about the odd-ball in their midst. But I knew it would be another story if I made a habit of it, this vengeful flaunting of convention. Still, at the last moment, I couldn't resist giving the fraternal bear one more little poke in the eye; so I knotted my scenic cravat and donned my stylish jacket for what I assumed would probably be their final outing, squared my padded shoulders, and went to dinner.

Predictably, the brethren were not impressed. They likened me to Mortimer Snerd and Clem Kadiddlehopper, and somebody theorized that I had come back with too much Kentucky on me, and would need to be quarantined for a few days. It was becoming obnoxiously clear to me that, in the opinion of these noble sons of the southern soil, there were few life-forms lower than a country bumpkin. I went along with the joke—having started it, I had little choice—but I was enjoying it less and less as the dinner hour wore on, and not at all by the time it was over.

Afterward, as I walked back to the dorm, these indignities still irked me, and I grew dimly mindful, like an oyster's first awareness of the annoying grain of sand that is destined to become its most prized possession, of a tiny nugget of that other kind of grit—the kind that makes a person do what he damn well pleases—lodged in some remote corner of my Inner Man. And a nacreous little resolution was already composing itself around it, to the following effect: tomorrow, I would wreak further vengeance upon the sonsabitches; tomorrow, no matter what, I would wear these goddamn clothes again.

In fact, I wore the offending finery the next day, and again the next day, and again the day after that. I don't know exactly why I did this, but it was like smoking; once I started I couldn't quit, or at any rate I didn't want to. By Friday of that week, the weather had turned too warm for the blue cords, so I replaced them with nondescript khakis, but otherwise my exterior person remained obdurately the same. Saturday mornings for freshmen were given over to ROTC drill (I declined Richard's proposal that I add the blue suedes to my Rotsie uniform), and the campus dress code didn't apply on weekends, so I had a few hours to air out my jacket. By Monday morning, it was ready for another week on duty.

And another, and another, and yet another ... Indeed, for five more weeks I strode the Spoonbred grounds in this distinctive attire like a very Ish Kabibble—long enough to attain a dubious sort of modest celebrity for myself as a public character. For a brief moment in history, I ranked right up there with the World's Longest Concrete Footbridge and the fully articulated skeleton of General Spoonbred's famous stallion, Peckerhead (then—as now—perpetually standing at stud in a glass display case outside the dean of students' office), among the sights not to be missed on our picturesque campus. And the undeniable truth is that—especially after a summer of exploring the dark heart of anonymity in DC—I was thoroughly enjoying my little moment of notoriety. For the first time in my life, I could be blithely oblivious to how other people saw me—which I took to mean that making a public nitwit of oneself has a lot in common with skulking about anonymously … and is, on balance, a lot more fun. I was discovering that eccentricity, like any other virtue, is its own reward.

But of course my brother SOBs regarded me not as the dashing renegade nonconformist I fancied myself but rather as a public embarrassment, a redheaded stepchild, a floater in the fraternal punch bowl. I was shunned—positively shunned, I tell you! Vengeance was mine!

By the last week of classes—dead week, as it was ominously denominated—I was the house pariah, a ghostly presence in a goofy getup. The brothers, having pretty thoroughly disowned me, had come around to putting up with me as a sort of household mendicant, a pitiable mongrel that came skulking around during the dinner hour, hoping for a handout. The dress code was suspended during dead week and finals week, fortunately for me, because by then my jacket was in tatters. (I'd been obliged to rip the lining out of it as the spring weather continued to warm. But the beleaguered garment had served me well and faithfully in my time of need, so I gave it my blessing when

I finally consigned it to the trash bin—along with, regrettably, my priceless cravat, the faux–Thomas Benton masterwork I had personally enhanced with a Pollockian spatter of gravy stains.) On the last Saturday morning of dead week, our ROTC unit celebrated itself with a grand parade, complete with an authentic one-star brigadier general of the United States Army dispatched all the way from Fort Leonard Wood, Missouri, to inspect us; and my gallant commander Lt. Whistledick personally designated me (along with a dumpy, bandy-legged kid I'll call Pvt. Bobbin, who waddled in a disconcertingly unmilitary manner when he marched) to stand guard at the gateway of the parade ground during these exercises, ostensibly to keep stray dogs off the field. Throughout the parade, I yearned in vain for some nearsighted pooch to wander along and mistake Lt. Whistledick's leg for a fire hydrant, while Pvt. Bobbin and I saluted from afar.

Regrettably, that didn't happen; nonetheless, the lieutenant's comeuppance was almost at hand. To wit: The ROTC brain trust had ordered all cadets to return their uniforms to government custody on Thursday afternoon of finals week, a duty I anticipated with unbridled enthusiasm, not least because I'd get back the twenty-five-dollar deposit my dad had put down on it, 'way last fall. The uniform had to be complete, which mine was, but my roommate, Richard, had taken his flimsy little government-issue, one-size-fits-all nylon raincoat home to Connecticut over spring break, and on the way back, it seemed, he'd left it on the Greyhound. The raincoat, a tiny affair that folded into a pad scarcely larger than a pocket handkerchief, was so insignificant (and so ineffectual) that Richard hadn't even missed it until now. But without it, he stood to forfeit his entire deposit, a loss he could ill afford, having budgeted every penny of the wayward twenty-five dollars for his Greyhound ticket home again.

So when I got back to the dorm after my Thursday morning French final (another C-minus in the offing there), I found Richard at his desk, bitterly lamenting his evanescent capital. His uniform, sans raincoat, was all nicely laid out across his bunk, ready for the quartermaster.

"God damn it to h-e-double-l! Twenty-five dollars and the crappy goddamn thing won't even turn water! What kinda godless atheistic commie government charges a person twenty-five goddamn dollars for one crappy little goddamn ..."

As he went on in this vein, losing more of his religion with every epithet, I glanced out the window, where I happened to spot, among the scholars scurrying hither and yon across the courtyard below, the plump, plucky figure of Lt. Whistledick, nee Balch, humping along toward the Jeff Davis Classroom Building like he was late (I could only hope) for an important exam. Richard, following my gaze, saw him too, and cordially included him in his blasphemies. Richard had his own beef with Lt. Balch, dating way back to a wintry Saturday morning in January, when our platoon was practicing its moves with dummy M-1 rifles, and the doughty lieutenant (speaking of dummies) somehow bollixed his commands during the inspection procedure and left half his troops holding back their weapon's spring-loaded clip mechanism with frozen hands while he embarked on a leisurely stroll through the ranks, making a great show of minutely examining each pseudo-weapon ... until, inevitably, one by one, guys began giving up and letting the goddamn thing fly, and the sharp *clack!* of steel bolts slamming home ricocheted here and there throughout the platoon, not infrequently accompanied by a yelp of pain when some poor sap—there you are, Richard!— left his hapless right thumb in the chamber an instant too long and the bolt whacked it like a tack hammer, whacked it so smartly that even now, months later, when Richard makes a pistol of his hand and points it at Whistledick down there crossing the courtyard and says "Pow!", the nail of his upraised right thumb is still mostly an inky purple bruise.

"Y'know," he mused, blowing invisible smoke off his fingertip, "officers don't turn in their uniforms till Saturday morning."

We sat there in silence for a few moments, while Richard waited for that to sink in. The halls of the dorm were quiet; everybody was at lunch, or taking an exam, or studying in the library. Neither of us needed to be reminded that as of Saturday morning, Richard would be on the Greyhound to Danbury, and I'd be on the train to Maysville—nor had we forgotten that, because at Spoonbred the omnipotent, omnipresent honor system took precedence over any trifling concerns about personal privacy, there were no locked doors in the dorm. Hmmm. I was getting the picture, and it prominently featured Lt. Balch.

"If memory serves," I mused, with all the innocence I could muster (not much), "I do believe the Whistle is an officer."

"This is true," Richard said, "this is very true." He rose from his desk chair and stepped to the door, opened it a crack, listened, then cautiously leaned out and peered up and down the hallway. He looked back at me, put his finger to his lips, and slipped out the door. I stayed at the window, keeping an eye on the now-empty courtyard; nothing was stirring. After only a couple of minutes, Richard came back, closed the door quietly behind him, and triumphantly brandished a small olive-drab nylon packet.

"How about that," he chuckled, tossing the raincoat onto his bunk, alongside the uniform. "I must've left it in Whistle's dresser drawer."

VIII. My Crazy, Mixed-Up Father

My father died of lung cancer and heart disease in the summer of 1962, and since his presence has loomed so large in this story, we'll end it with his passing. But that melancholy time comes a full ten years after my de-matriculation from Spoonbred U, and in narrator years, that could turn out to be a very long, tedious interim indeed—especially if one is stuck (as you are) with a narrator who doesn't seem to know when to get on with the goddamn story, fer crissakes. So now I'm going to take my own advice, and proceed with all the deliberate speed I can manage.

I spent that first post-Spoonbred summer working as a rodman on a surveying crew for the Kentucky state highway department. It was sometimes hot, sweaty, demanding work, but there was a lot of downtime too, when we holed up in the back office, out of view of the taxpayers, and played cards, or pitched pennies, or otherwise fornicated the canine. I somehow got on a Sinclair Lewis tear that summer, and read both *Main Street* and *Babbitt* sitting on dusty cardboard boxes stuffed with ancient highway department documents, cowering from public scrutiny in that musty old back room. I also read *The Naked and the Dead* and *From Here to Eternity* on my own time, and the new teenage sensation *Catcher in the Rye*, and of course I continued my study of the immortal Erskine Caldwell, which I still pursued while standing at the paperback rack in Kilgus's Drugstore. I had no idea, certainly, that there existed any such phenomenon as a literary movement called realism, but if anyone had asked me what I liked about these books, I would've said it was that they were "realistic." As soon as I got a good start on my career as a freelance writer up at Miami, I intended to write something so scandalously realistic it would probably make me as famous as what's-his-name, the guy who wrote *Forever Amber*. (Yeah, yeah, I Googled him too—so don't tell me, I *know* the dude's pen name is Kathleen.)

But I threatened to kick out the jams in this rambling meditation, and the moment for doing so is at hand. Fortunately, my narrative can now proceed by leaps and bounds, because I've already written (dare I say exhaustively?) about almost everything of consequence that transpired in my life during those next ten years, in three or four books (as well as elsewhere in this one). As I take it, this leaves me at liberty to summarize my adventures more or less at will, with the understanding that if you really want more details, you can look it up yourself.

Miami turned out fine. I bumbled through one more ex-
cruciating year of ROTC, and then managed to evade the
clutches of Miss Alma Potts and the Selective Service for the
next two years, thanks to the hitherto inconceivable fact that
over those six semesters, my grades improved, incrementally ·
but inexorably, semester after semester, keeping me one step
ahead of Miss Alma the whole way. My friend Ned had married not long after I arrived, and was all preoccupied with
becoming a grown-up during those years; but I had slogged
through a whole year at Spoonbred to get to Miami, and now
that I was there, I was determined to take full advantage of
its amenities. For the next three years, I reveled knee-deep in
three-two beer and the enlivening presence of all those naked tree frogs, and took all the creative writing courses the
law allowed, wherein I wrote stories about the day the hogs
et Cousin Junior, stories so realistic they would make Erskine
Caldwell retch with admiration. I even chose to major in so-
ciology, on the shaky assumption that it would enhance my
professional credentials as an unblinking, gimlet-eyed realist.

After Miami, with Miss Alma still nipping at my heels, I
somehow weaseled my way into Wallace Stegner's graduate
creative writing program at Stanford, and then weaseled my
way right back out again after only two academic quarters,
having reverted to my old C-minus habits. I knew this little
setback meant that Miss Alma would soon be taking renewed
interest in me, so I outfoxed her by hauling ass back to Kentucky and immediately scurrying down to Lexington to en-
roll as an English major in grad school at the state university.
Even with my head start (such as it was) at Stanford, it took me

another two full years to wrest an MA from UK's begrudging pedagogues. I met and married my first wife, Kit, during those two years at UK, and together we ran with a fast crowd that included my raffish classmates Wendell Berry, James Baker Hall, and Gurney Norman—my new brotherhood. Midway through the second year, Miss Alma, breathless after almost seven years of hot pursuit, caught up with me at last and required me to submit to a pre-induction physical. I answered the call, armed with a note from a pacifistically inclined allergist of my acquaintance, who attested (like a presentiment of Donald Trump's podiatrist) that my annual bouts of hay fever constituted "chronic asthmatic allergy," and lo, they turned me down and sent me back!

Finally, in the spring of '58, after one epic fail, I passed the UK master's oral exam and graduated with an MA so lame it should've come with its own handicapped parking permit. If I couldn't land a college teaching job, that MA wouldn't qualify me to be a junior high school crosswalk guard. I had exactly one live job application in the offing, for a freshman comp instructorship in a remote educational outpost somewhere in Oregon. But that prospect seemed almost laughably improbable, and otherwise I had no prospects at all.

I was also laboring, at the time, under a secret yearning to go in for *la vie Bohème* in some capacity or another. Specifically, I wanted to take off with my new bride to some hipster pad (those accommodations being the hottest thing going, according to *Life* magazine) in Greenwich Village or San Francisco or maybe even on the Left Bank of the Rue de la Paix in downtown Paris, France, where I would set up shop as a sullen, brooding, existentialist freelance writer, a trade for which I wouldn't be needing no damn piddle-ass MA in English anyhow, thank you very much. This was all a pipe dream, of course—I was to a freelance writer what Lt. Whistledick was to Gen. MacArthur, and for that matter I wasn't all that sure what "existential" meant, either—but I had the sullen, brooding part down cold, and I was in no mood to be trifled with. Such was my state of mind when my father decided—remember this?—to throw that big launching party for his brand new houseboat at ... Kamp Fucking Kadet!

The location was a complete coincidence; the military school had long since sold the property to a local sportsmen's club, which renamed it something like "Ye Olde Rod 'n' Reel Retreat" and rented it out for private riverside parties and events. As far as I know, my parents weren't aware that it had ever been Kamp Kadet, but I recognized it right away. There was an overgrown putting green where our old softball backstop had been, and clay pigeon throws had replaced the archery range, but it was Kamp Kadet all right. I could almost hear the hoofbeats of Cap'n Batshit's imaginary horse.

My parents were generous hosts, and they both enjoyed giving parties, so this one promised to be something of a blowout. They invited seventy-five or eighty friends and business associates, hired a Lexington caterer and a bartender, and hauled in enough country ham and beaten biscuits and devilled eggs to feed Spoonbred's army and enough alcohol to drown a water buffalo—on account of which my memory of the occasion is like an ancient home movie, so shaky and out of focus and fragmented and riddled with incoherent jump cuts that, even now, replaying it in my head makes me queasy, like watching *The Blair Witch Project* was said to do. Still, I'm grateful for the lapses; would that I could also forget the parts that I remember.

Ordinarily, returning to places that were familiar in one's childhood is startling for the way everything seems to have shrunk, but this time everything else had stayed pretty much the same, and it was me who was diminished. The Rod 'n' Reel guys had preserved the old main building, and the bar at my dad's party was set up in the very dining hall where, one day at suppertime fifteen years before, the lionhearted Cap'n Batshit had pushed my ten-year-old bunk-mate Dougie's face into a bowl of buttterscotch pudding, in order to toughen him up and make him combat-ready and teach him not to say he really didn't care for butterscotch pudding. Each time I visited the bar, which occurred all too frequently that afternoon, I envisioned meek little Dougie sitting there with a giant cow pie of butterscotch pudding smeared from ear to ear.

But see, it was the *bar*, after all, so I *had* to keep coming back. My dad, meanwhile, had taken up his own station there as the genial host, and was holding court with his guests and pounding down the Old Charter, jauntily sporting a white yachtsman's cap someone had given him in celebration of his new toy—which, by the way, had spontaneously material- ized down at the dock somehow when I wasn't looking, that monstrous white floating shoebox with the matching twenty- five-horse Evinrude outboards, bobbing down there in the shallows. If there was a launching ceremony—and there must have been—it has vanished into an alcohol-induced haze, slipping away into the fog like a ghost ship. What I do recall, painfully, is that, in the presence of a group of partiers that doubtless included any number of perfectly nice Standard Oil of Kentucky executives and other important personages, my dad ordered me once too often to go park some cars or get some ice or perform some equally innocuous task—me, a married man, a master of the arts!—and I got all huffy and stamped my little foot and stalked away, indignantly bleating that, goddammit, I was *not* his cabin boy.

I was ten years old again, I was back at Kamp Kadet, and my dad was channeling Cap'n Batshit—except this time the ten-year-old was also twenty-four, thoroughly a-slosh with Dutch courage, and seething with false certainties and fugitive resentments. I have no recollection at all of what happened next, so let's assume that I crept away in ignominy and disrepute and somehow found our car and went to sleep in the back seat, and Kit drove us home hours later.

Well, that's the short version of what would turn out to be my last real contretemps with my dad, and it's the only version you're going to get. Suffice it to say that this was not my finest hour. My fervent hope was—and still is—that my dad had been even more schnockered than I was, and that for him the entire episode, including the parts I couldn't remember myself, had swirled away down the memory hole. At any rate, neither he nor I ever mentioned it. "Talking things over" just wasn't something we ordinarily did; instead, we generally communicated by means of alternating sullen silences, punctuated by the occasional meaningful grunt. But regardless of whether my dad ever thought of it again, I certainly did, and do; and every time, I cringe and look away.

I have referred (more than once, I'm afraid) to my "lame" master's degree; yet just a few days after the lamentable launching party, that jake-legged honorific, its impairments notwithstanding, would land me a job as Instructor of Freshman Composition at Oregon State College, in Corvallis, where I would teach prescriptive grammar for the next four years—which will ultimately bring us, in case you haven't been counting, to 1962, the year my father died. As usual, though, that requires a smidge of backstory:

American business was booming throughout the 1950s, and the famous rising tide that lifts all boats had given the towboat business a nice little boost as well. The Triangle Towing Company prospered apace, and my dad and his business partner, Ned's uncle Pete, enjoyed the hell out of their success. They were both country boys, self-made men, and living large was their reward. They played the ponies at Keeneland and Churchill Downs, and eventually bought their own racehorse, a gelding claimer by the counterintuitive name of Hypo's Hope. (Actually, Hypo ran in the money several times, and earned enough to keep himself in oats during his tenure in the Triangle stable.) In the line of duty, my dad and Pete played high-stakes poker with business and political pals in Louisville and Frankfort and Pittsburgh, and stoically undertook the rigors of traveling wherever the towing business took them—destinations including such remote outposts of Ohio River commerce as Las Vegas, New Orleans, and New York City.

Many years after my father's death, I heard an ancient rumor that he and Pete had installed sumptuous private staterooms on the *Elisha Wood*, and sometimes entertained lady friends on little cruises. And now I'm filing that away under Certain Things I Don't Wanna Think About Ever Again. Remind me of it at your peril.

So. One morning a few days after that lamentable party, when I had abandoned all hope to such an extent that I'd even briefly stood before the Gates of Hell (a.k.a. the office of the Board of Education) trying to persuade myself to apply for a position as a substitute high school English teacher, I picked up the mail and ... Holy Moly, I was off to Oregon! Which is on the West Coast! Where California is!

At UK, I had sustained my literary credentials mostly by recycling old undergraduate and Stanford stories, and by the time I got to Oregon, my dedication to the actual task of writing had fallen woefully short of steadfast. Indeed, throughout my first couple of years there, it was essentially moribund, though I wasn't ready to admit it yet, even to myself. I had my hands full just maintaining the fiction that I was writing fiction.

It wasn't in the cards, unfortunately, that my dad and I would ever give ourselves a chance to enjoy the rewards a truly flourishing relationship would have brought us; we were far too wary of each other to allow for that. But during my and Kit's years in Oregon, we bounced back to Kentucky regularly, and my dad and I gradually found ways to accommodate our differences when circumstances brought us together. We still made it a matter of principle to disagree, of

course, about everything from presidential politics (his pref-
erences would've made Senator Kermode look like a Bolshe-
vik, whereas I was partial to that fierce old wild west Wobbly,
Oregon's own Wayne Morris) to the fashionable resurgence of
male facial hair. (In homage to, among aforementioned others,
my new literary heroes Kerouac and his unshorn Beat associates, I even cultivated my first moustache, a waxed, Daliesque
adornment to go with my DA hairdo. My dad, in what I had to
admit was a pretty good line, characterized it as "a basketball
moustache: five on a side.")

All that notwithstanding, he and I were getting along better over time. At spring break of our second year in Oregon,
Kit and I even undertook a family trip with my parents down
the coast to San Francisco, where, according to the popular
press, these Beatnik persons were becoming both a plague
and a tourist attraction, a traveling freak show that had taken
up residence in the town square and stubbornly refused to
move along. They tended to congregate, it was said, in such
North Beach resorts as City Lights Bookstore and Vesuvio and
the Co-Existence Bagel Shop and Mike's Pool Hall, a few of
which I was already slightly acquainted with, from my earlier
fifteen minutes at Stanford. Nowadays, I found, busloads of
rubbernecking tourists cruised the neighborhood, so, lest we
be mistaken for another gaggle of squares, I generously volun-
teered to lead our little party on a private tour. Kit and my parents dutifully trailed me around while I held forth on the Beat
aesthetic as I understood it (which, needless to say, I didn't)
and schooled them (despairingly) in the subtleties of hipster
patois ("No no, Mom, 'hipster,' not 'hepster'!") and explained

how it was all related to the underlying existential oversoul of, you know, everything else. At my urging, they sampled unpotable mead at Vesuvio and unpalatable coffee at Enrico's, and listened patiently to uninspired poetry declaimed by an unwashed street poet outside City Lights.

"Real George, man!" our bard's lone remaining admirer declared as we moved on. "That's some crazy mixed-up jive!"

My dad heroically endured the whole charade with a minimum of head-shaking and low-key grumbling until I steered us to the Purple Onion, a nightspot recently made famous by Lenny Bruce's abrasive rants. Lenny wasn't on the bill that night (a great blessing, I see now), but we were graced instead by that comedian who sang "Go Take a Ship for Yourself," the one who inspired my dad's indignation, and precipitated our hasty departure. My dad insisted afterward that he'd hustled us out because the song was morally offensive to the ladies ("Take a canoe, take a kayak, take a raft," the comedian had sung. "If you can't take a ship, take a great big healthy craft …"), but Kit told me privately that she and my mom had both thought the guy's act was hilarious, and that my mom had said she couldn't imagine why my dad raised such a heecack about it.

During those first years up in Oregon, meanwhile, something quite unexpected had entered my life. For at Oregon State, in that howling wilderness way up yonder in the upper left-hand corner of civilization as we know it, I had fallen into a nest of versemongers. Among my new colleagues were no fewer than five accomplished young lyric poets—John Haislip, Robert Huff, Fred Staver, Melvin La Follette, and Gene

Lundahl—each of whom, like me, was teaching four sections of freshman comp, and each of whom was fairly bursting with the music of language. (I should mention too that we were all inspired, en masse, by the mere presence of yet another colleague, Bernard Malamud, who was quietly writing masterful fiction right down the hall.) My new friends and I toiled by day down in the boiler room of language, parsing away among the gerunds and participles and infinitives, and then, in our time off, we reveled in its ineffable power. As a group, these were the best drinking companions I ever had. Remember that bouncy little 1950s animated cartoon character named Gerald McBoing-Boing, whose every utterance was a sound effect, a lion's roar or a passing freight train or the milkman's clip-clop or an orchestral symphony? My Oregon poet friends, a voluble colloquy of Dylan Thomases, were like Gerald; when they opened their mouths to talk, lyric poetry spilled forth, language resonant with metaphor and music. Two or three times a week we'd hit one of the downtown beer parlors after school, and the talk was always far more intoxicating than the beer. Sometimes it was like listening to birdsong, raucous and wild but joyously musical in every semiquaver. Or, to try another admixture of metaphors, language was to these guys as pigment is to a painter, or stone to a sculptor; an almost palpable, almost living substance that was theirs to shape at will.

These revelations, such as they were, gradually set off in our Gimlet-Eyed Young Realist a certain yearning to cut his Inner Poet a little slack. I spent my second summer in Oregon writing a new story in a far more venturesome voice, a romantically artsy threnody front-loaded with wretched excess (along with a new, overweening enthusiasm for assonance and alliteration, I had suddenly developed a three-adjective habit that would choke Francis the Talking Mule), despite which, to my astonishment and delight, the story was accepted right away and published in a hip, nationally distributed San Francisco quarterly. Catching a little tailwind from that, I started a second, more ambitious story, which quickly ballooned into a novella, and suddenly, as the spring term of 1962 came to an end, I had a New York agent, a contract for a book of stories, a promotion (Think of that! Me, Mr. C-minus, an assistant professor!), and, best of all, beginning in the autumn, a Stegner Fellowship to Stanford. I was going back to Stanford!

There was even a cherry atop this toothsome confection: thanks to kind recommendations by my Oregon State colleague Bernard Malamud and my erstwhile Stanford teacher Malcolm Cowley, I'd been granted a residency fellowship to Yaddo, the artists' colony in Saratoga Springs, New York, for the coming month of June. As you might imagine, I was walking on air; by the time Kit and I and our frisky, bright-eyed two-year-old firstborn, Kristen, went back to Kentucky for a visit before I moved on to Yaddo, I could've flown in on my own power, on wings of gossamer.

My parents, flush with their own successes, had gone home to Bracken County the year before, and bought a house near Brooksville that my mother had loved and longed for all her life, a stately, white-columned antebellum country manor that General Spoonbred himself would have envied. Unhappily, however, my dad's health hadn't thrived in concurrence with his business affairs; he'd been hospitalized a couple of times by mild heart attacks over the years, and he'd packed on too many pounds around the middle. And of course he still drank too much and smoked too much—but then so did I, so I could hardly fault him for that. His early morning coughing spells now lasted till noon, but he couldn't quit smoking. He'd recently tried Tareytons (the filters were little tubes packed with grains of activated charcoal, like tiny shotgun shells), and then Sanos (so vile the aftertaste alone would gag a turkey buzzard), and settled at last on Kents, with their celebrated "Micronite" filter. Considering that Micronite was eventually revealed to consist largely of asbestos, it was no surprise that Kents hadn't done much for his cough.

Around the time my folks moved back to Bracken County, a Lexington friend of mine had suddenly needed to find a home for his big, handsome boxer pup, Boggles, so we made some arrangements, and Boggles moved to Bracken County too. Pete, my dad's longtime partner, was himself in failing health by then, and in his absence, Boggles took over as my dad's constant companion and running mate. My dad's last car, his final tribute to planned obsolescence, was a white 1960 Lincoln Continental with white leather upholstery and Dag-mars on the front bumper. Boggles immediately took charge of the front seat of the Lincoln, riding shotgun in fine weather with his big head hanging out the passenger side window, tak-ing the air as, together, he and my dad cruised the byways and back roads of Bracken County.

So when Kit and Kris and I arrived for our visit before my month at Yaddo, my dad and I each had shiny new acqui-sitions to our credit. As I happily trotted out my fellowships and whatnot, I saw that he took as much pride in them as I did, and that he was basking in the presence of his first grandchild. Apart from the state of his health—which was even more precarious than we knew—it was a promising beginning.

That evening after dinner, he and Boggles and Kris and I strolled around outside, admiring the property and the grand old house, Kris toddling along at my father's side, holding his hand. As we were going back inside, we stopped in the driveway while Boggles put his personal imprimatur on the right front whitewall of the Continental, as if he meant to make sure everybody knew just whose car it really was. My dad stood there in the porch light for a long moment, taking in the scene with evident satisfaction.

"Wellsir," he said finally, "I told 'em I wasn't coming back till I had the biggest house and the biggest car and the biggest dog in Bracken County. And by god"—he chuckled, and paused just long enough to let me know that, behind the boast, he was mostly kidding—"by god, son, I got 'er."

—

On the twenty-ninth of my thirty days at Yaddo, Kit called to tell me that my dad had been hospitalized for exploratory surgery, and had been diagnosed with inoperable lung cancer. The following morning, I caught the soonest, most direct flight to Lexington. Kit met my plane and drove me straight to the hospital, where I found my dad lying, alone, in a semi-darkened room. His eyes were closed, and he looked so wan and wasted that at first I feared I'd come too late. While

I hesitated at the foot of his bed, he stirred, then opened his eyes and murmured, in a whispery voice enfeebled by pain and apprehension, "Oh, Ed!"

Just that, just two tiny, whispered syllables fraught with dismay, yet they also affirmed with lucent clarity his surprise and delight that I was there, and I was immeasurably grateful for them. Instantly, it seemed, all our petty enmities and animosities were banished, and in their place there remained only regret and affection and forgiveness. He would live for four more days before his weakened heart gave out, but that would be our final private moment, and the one that has stayed with me, now, for almost sixty years.

But before I let this narrative maunder along to its inevitable melancholy conclusion, I need to tie up a few loose ends: Grieving my father's death, Boggles pined away and followed him six months later. Pete's health was also failing; he retired from the towing business, and died not long thereafter. As you will perhaps recall, my mother couldn't swim; she was, in fact, terrified of water, and she loathed every miserable minute she'd been obliged to spend on that houseboat during the four years she and my dad owned it. When he died, she sold it with almost unseemly haste, after a barely decent interval. In 1968, on my thirty-sixth birthday, I quit smoking, held my breath for the next four years, took up the tobacco habit again for a few years in my early forties, and quit for good in 1974. My mother, with the help of my late dad's older brother, Don, a widowed Cincinnati realtor whom she eventually married, continued to operate Triangle Towing successfully for another fifteen years or so, till around 1978. They sold the Bracken County house in 1980 and moved to Cincinnati, where Don, a lifelong smoker, died of lung cancer in the tenth year of their marriage. Ned, throughout a hugely successful career on Wall Street, remained my dearest friend until the day he died of, yes, lung cancer in 2003. My mother, on the other hand, smoked a few cigarettes every day for the rest of her long, healthy life, completely undeterred despite being twice widowed by tobacco, and died at eighty-eight of age-related heart failure. Tee many martoonies proved the undoing of Uncle Void, and the same palliative eventually took down Aunt Pidge as well.

One more loose end, and then I'll turn this yarn over to posterity, to knit of it what it will: It so happened that back in 1980, when she and Don were preparing to make their move to Cincinnati, my mom came across the suitcase my dad had carried on his travels with Pete, back when they were flying high. In the otherwise empty suitcase were an old menu from a once-famous Greenwich Village steakhouse called O. Henry's, and a large, well-executed charcoal sketch of my dad, nicely framed and under glass, signed by an artist who called himself "Primitivo." It was inscribed "your mixed-up father" in my dad's hand, and datelined "NYC '59"—the same year we had made that family pilgrimage to ogle the San Francisco Beatniks. It occurred to me that the "NYC" in the dateline suggested that Ned might have been involved somehow, so I called him and we compared recollections, and pieced together this scenario:

In 1959, Hypo's Hope had run in the fall meet at Aqueduct, where he again finished in the money, and got claimed.

My dad and Pete were on hand to see him run, and, having cashed in, returned to their Manhattan hotel ready for a celebratory evening in the city. My dad had been telling Pete about our little foray earlier that year among the heathen Beatnik hordes of San Francisco, and Pete had a hankering to see some of these exotic specimens for himself, so they called Pete's nephew Ned and asked him where, at a safe distance, the famous Greenwich Village Beatniks could be observed in their natural habitat. Try O. Henry's Steak House, Ned suggested; the steaks aren't bad, and in that neighborhood you can't swing a cat without hitting a Beatnik.

So that explained the menu, and as to "Primitivo," we conjectured that the self-appointed artist-in-residence of the College of Complexes must have been one of those Village humbugs who affected berets and French accents, and kept themselves in pocket change and cocktails by knocking out souvenir sketches or caricatures of the tourists.

The guy was good, though. The portrait is by far the best likeness I have of my dad; in the picture, he is handsome and composed, and seems to be looking to the future with steely determination—exactly the sort of image of himself that I would've thought he would enjoy. Thereby begging the question: Why had he hidden it away as though it were something shameful or embarrassing?

I could only conclude that he'd had second thoughts about his inscription: *"your mixed-up father."* Looking at it in his hotel room by the sobering morning-after light, he must've decided that it sounded like an apology, a capitulation—whereas I heard only a gingerly but nonetheless tender acknowledgement that, amid all the pleasures and diversions of New York City, I was on his mind. Even as he sat for the picture, he was formulating the words that, minutes later, he would be inscribing on it.

What I have, then—as surely as if Primitivo, that unsung visionary genius, had drawn a thought balloon above his subject's head with my own picture inside it—is a portrait of my dad in the very act of thinking lovingly and hopefully of me. Knowing that, I wouldn't trade it for the *Mona Lisa*, enigmatic smile and all.

Tony

MY FIRST BOOK (AND ONLY NOVEL), *THE NATURAL MAN*, WAS a long time coming; it finally arrived in the spring of 1983, when I was fifty. The book had already been greeted by several very heartening advance reviews, and my publisher had lined up a series of readings and book signings for me, the first of which was somewhere in Northern Kentucky, across the Ohio from Cincinnati. (I can't quite recall the venue; perhaps a bookstore or public library in Covington or Newport or Fort Thomas.) To my surprise and delight, two of my favorite schoolmates of long ago showed up for the event: my grade-school inamorata Jackie Perkins Hamilton, who had grown up to be a reporter for the *Bracken County News*, our home-town weekly, and James Hubert "Shoobie" Hamilton (no relation to Jackie), who had been my best friend throughout my boyhood.

My novel is set in a small northeastern Kentucky town ("Needmore") modeled on Brooksville, the county seat of Bracken County; its title character, a hulking teenager called Monk McHorning, is based in part on a burly, street-wise city kid named Paul "Tony" Maloney, who had come to

Brooksville from Newport in 1945 as a fifteen-year-old basketball prodigy. Tony was a power player, a banger; yet he had
a kind of lumbering grace, and what he lacked in finesse he
more than made up for in main strength and truculence. In
little Brooksville (population around six hundred fifty, then
and now) Tony seemed larger than life, Gulliver among the
Lilliputians, a monumental presence. But he wasn't considered "college material" (whatever that may be), and after high
school he joined the army, at which point I lost track of him
for many years.

In the novel, Monk is befriended by a classmate, Harry
Eastep, who earns the irascible newcomer's grudging respect
by ghostwriting his English themes for him, and who is pretty
obviously my fictional alter ego. Monk and Harry each leave
Needmore in the late 1940s to find their own separate ways
in the larger world, just as Tony Maloney and I had each left
Brooksville around that same time—and their paths, like
ours, were never to cross again.

(*The Natural Man* is a work of fiction, of course, so I ad-
justed the biographical content according to the narrative
requirements of my imagination; in reality I was a couple of
years younger than Tony, and I wouldn't become his nomi-
nal amanuensis until several eons later, when I finally wrote
my novel. I should mention too that Monk's character is also
drawn in approximately equal part from my late friend Carlos
"Little Enis" Toadvine, "The World's Greatest Left-Handed
Upside-Down Guitar Player," and from my old Maysville pal
Willie Gordon Ryan, to whom the book is dedicated.)

By 1983, when my book was published, I'd heard some-where that in the intervening years, Tony, after a stint in the military, had returned to Newport and become a solid citizen there. It even occurred to me that he might show up for my reading, a possibility that was, on the one hand, exhilarating—I regarded Monk McHorning, after all, as the true hero of my novel (or, if you will, the antihero)—and, on the other, a bit unsettling, inasmuch as Tony (still a pretty rough customer, I supposed) just might find my portrayal of Monk's manners and morals and Outer Primate not alto-gether to his satisfaction.

My old pals Shoobie and Jackie were among the first arriv-als for the reading. Shoobie, who then lived in Fort Thomas, brought with him a clipping from the previous day's Northern Kentucky edition of the *Cincinnati Enquirer*:

Alas, it was an obituary, a rather substantial one, head-lined "Paul A. Maloney, GI in 'Life.'" Tony had indeed passed away just days before, after a too-short but exemplary life in the area; a heavy equipment operator by trade, he'd been a union official, a Kentucky Colonel, a deputy sheriff (think of that!), a father of three, a stalwart member of the PTA—and he was a war hero! As a wounded, battle-weary GI in the ear-liest days of the Korean conflict, he'd been the subject of an iconic photograph in *Life* magazine. Hardly the sort of resume I would've expected from the obstreperous Rough Customer who (according to Shoobie, who had been his teammate) once left an opposing center standing on the basketball court in tears.

And as if that weren't irony enough, I was simultaneously reminded of yet another extraordinary coincidence, or set of coincidences. For in the novel, photos of Monk McHorning, Tony's doppelganger, also figure prominently; his picture appears in (yes!) the *Cincinnati Enquirer* no fewer than three times—once when, at the tender age of twelve, he almost succeeds in joining the US Army, once on the sports page during his brief but glorious tenure on the hardwood down in Needmore, and one last time in the early 1970s, accompanying a story announcing his death (by fragging) in Vietnam. He is the novel's hero mostly by virtue of his having scorned a point-shaving scheme, rejecting it not because he's incorruptible (far from it), but rather just because he refuses to be owned.

I've long since forgotten what portion of my novel I read that afternoon, but I daresay it was something scurrilous. It's just that kind of book. Yet Jackie, bless her heart, chose to pay no attention at all to any of that; her endearing report in the *Bracken County News* affectionately featured the fact that I was wearing patched jeans, which she took to be a satisfactory indication that I hadn't started putting on airs.

Anyhow, even though I could never have predicted that Tony Maloney would turn out to be such a splendid ornament to polite society, I'd like to think he'd certainly have rebuffed out of hand any proposition to sell out, just as Monk McHorning does, and for exactly the same reason. That, after all, would be the Way of the Hero.

Me and Gurney Goes
Out on the Town

AS MY KENTUCKY WRITER FRIEND GURNEY NORMAN'S press agent and chief flack for, lo, these sixty years now, I've accumulated a headful of anecdotes about his wanton, debauched, dissipated history—anecdotes that would certainly make him famous beyond his wildest dreams if I released them to the tabloids—but Gurney, having become inordinately concerned, in our mutual dotage, with protecting his cherished image as a paragon of virtue, absolutely forbids me from revealing the real hot stuff.

So here's an anecdote—a mostly true one, except for the parts I made up—describing an incident to which Gurney and I were eye witnesses, but in which neither of us participated in the least degree.

This would've been around 1986 or '87, I guess. I was teaching at UK, driving in to Lexington from Henry County a couple of times a week, and once in a while I'd spend the night at my UK colleague and life-long dear friend Gurney's place. And one of those times, Gurney and I decided, for some obscure reason, that we owed ourselves a boys' night out, and, for some even more obscure reason, that we should go forth

and regale ourselves among the lovely, lively B-girl go-go ladies at Boots Bar in the decrepit old Scott Hotel, where my late
pal Little Enis, the World's Greatest Left-handed Upside-down
Guitar Player (d. 1976), once reigned supreme.

Accordingly, we betook our imposing professorial selves
across town to Boots ("overlookin' the Southern Railroad
tracks," as Enis used to say), and a table in a large, darkened
room partly occupied by a little stage, its front lip doubling
as a makeshift bar or counter. There were half a dozen short
barstools lined up before it for especially devout patrons of
the arts, none of whom, it seemed, had arrived as yet. But a
handful of other customers, most of them men, hunkered
here and there like lonesome castaways at little table islands
out there in the smoky gloom. The jukebox was blaring Faron
Young's mournful "Pick Me Up on Your Way Down," and on
the stage an unprepossessing lady of indeterminate age, patriotically suited up in star-shaped pasties and star-spangled
mini-britches and sparkly spike-heeled shoes, was wearily
marching in place to the tune. Her essential nakedness notwithstanding, there wasn't really all that much to see.

It was, by and large, the same old Boots Bar, only without
Enis. Back in Enis's day, '72 or '73, Boots had been, not to put
too fine a point upon it, the employer of last resort for both aspiring and retiring go-go dancers, and that policy, it appeared,
was still operative.

"Crank it up, Marcella!" urged a voice out of the darkness.
"Shake that parkin' meter!"

Marcella flipped off her anonymous admirer and resolutely soldiered on till Faron had concluded his lament. Then,

teetering dangerously on her spikes, she clambered down from the stage by means of a tiny attached stepladder, flung some sort of filmy little baby-doll negligee about her narrow shoulders, picked up a tray, and clunked across the little dance floor to our table. We asked for a couple of beers.

"Whyn't y'all buy me a drink too, so I can set down a while," she said. "My feet's plumb wore out."

Gurney and I said we'd happily spring for the drink, and made room for her at the table.

"Well then," said Marcella, gesturing toward the table nearest ours, where a formidable-looking elderly lady sat glowering at us from beneath an oakum-colored wig, "well then, how about Mom?"

"Of course!" cried Gurney (secure in the knowledge that it wasn't his round anyhow). A beer for Mom by all means!

Marcella waved Mom over and slogged off to fetch the drinks. Gurney and I leapt to our several feet to hold Mom's chair while she laboriously repositioned her cumbrous person at our table. Marcella came back with the beer and a glass of some dark potion that passed itself off as a cocktail, and I dutifully ponied up.

"So," Marcella demanded of Mom when we were all situated at the table, "was that Randall a-hollerin'?"

"Yes, missy," Mom snapped, plumping herself up like a mother hen addressing an errant chick, "it was fucken Randall."

"That little s'rimp," Marcella growled through gritted teeth. "I'd like to smack his lips off."

By now Marcella had been replaced onstage by another

middle-aged young lady called Sugarbush, who was laboring away to the stirring jukebox strains of Jeannie C. Riley's
rendition of "Harper Valley PTA," a tune about as impossible
to dance to as "The Woody Woodpecker Song." But Sugarbush, a chunky blonde minimally tricked out in a G-string
and gold-tasseled pasties, was giving it her all, with a terpsi-
chorean interpretation of "Harper Valley PTA" that seemed
to involve stomping out untold numbers of tiny Harper Valley
hypocrites.

"Shake it, Sugar!" the fickle, faithless Randall called ec-
statically, out of the darkness. "Show us them biscuits!" Sugarbush obligingly turned her expansive backside to her admirer
and set it in motion, so that it jiggled like a generous dollop
of white-flour gravy—a commodity that, come to think of it,
was probably among its chief components.

Mom took a pretty long pull at her beer (there were glasses,
but Mom had not elected to decant) and again declared her
eternal enmity to Randall, a sentiment Marcella not only en-
dorsed with all her heart but also expanded to accommodate
a whole host of Randall's friends, neighbors, associates, and
second fucken cousins, and in the process called him every
species of insensitive lout she could think of off the top of her
head. Randall, it seemed, had done Marcella dirt somehow,
and—although the exact nature of his offense had perhaps
been lost to history—she and Mom sure as hell knew how to
hold a grudge, and they had this one by the short hairs.

The much-reviled Randall, meanwhile, having made
his way into the light, was now enthroned on one of the
squat barstools at the front of the stage, eye-level with the

aforementioned biscuits. As advertised, Randall was indeed a little shrimp, a shifty-looking Ratso Rizzo type except for the rank profusion of coarse black hair that spilled over his narrow shoulders and halfway down his back like a fuzzy prayer shawl. Professionally, Marcella told us, Randall was a stable hand at one of the local thoroughbred farms, where part of his job was tending the stall of a famous stallion. This had evidently given Randall the mistaken impression that his association with the celebrated horse made him, Randall, something of a celebrity himself, whereas in Marcella's humble opinion he didn't amount to a hickey on a slebberty's butt. Mom, her wig slightly askew, said she'd sure as hell drink to that, and did so, with alacrity and gusto.

Marcella was called away to wait on another table, and Sugarbush yielded the stage to Dixie, a tall, slender young woman who undertook a sort of stationary waltz with herself ("Kick out the jams, Slim!" Randall pleaded halfheartedly. "Lay it down and r-r-roll it out!") to some ethereal elevator music she alone was hearing ("She takes them old downer pills, poor thing," Mom confided), as the jukebox irrelevantly bellowed "Wake Me Up Before You Go-Go" at the top of its electronic lungs. Like her predecessors, Dixie had come before us pretty much *au naturel*, but her overall affect was so somnolent and detached that her entire unclothed presence slowly receded into Boots's ambient gloom.

And that's when Randall made the fateful—damn near fatal—mistake of shifting his attentions to what he supposed was a more promising venue for them, and thereby brought this whole unwieldy anecdote of mine to a swift and unexpected denouement. For it so happened that Marcella, coming back with her empty drink tray, was just then crossing the dance floor, and as she passed behind Randall's barstool, he noticed her and brayed, over his shoulder, "Whoa there, Table-grade!" and reached back to treat her to a complimentary pat on the rump.

But what Randall didn't know was that Marcella had already had it up to here with him, that fucken Randall, and she absolutely wasn't having any more. In the blink of an eye she whirled around and, adroitly dodging the affectionate swat, dealt old Randall a tremendous blow on his shaggy pate with the flat of her tray and rang it like a dinner bell. She chucked the tray aside and plunged both hands into Randall's mane and gave it a mighty yank and toppled him backward off his roost, and by the time he hit the floor she'd somehow got one of her spikes in hand and was vigorously applying it—*whack! whack! whack!*—about the head and shoulders of the cringing, cowering Randall. Finally she thrust her hands into his hair again and hauled him to his feet and marched him straight across the room and through the bar to the front door and pushed him out into the street and slammed the door behind him.

Her foe vanquished into ignominious exile, Marcella stumped back through the room on one spike heel, her negligee reduced to tatters by Randall's flailings, her star-spangled Wonder Woman regalia—what there was of it—on full display, her face alight in triumph, her fine blue eyes a-glint with steely Wonder Woman resolve. Dusting off her palms in the traditional "Job well done!" fashion, she sat back down to put on her other shoe. Gurney and Mom and I greeted her return with a spontaneous little round of applause, and were joined in that by two or three other Boots denizens who'd been roused from their torpor by the commotion.

"Well bless your heart, hon," Mom said proudly. "You done real fucken good."

Along about then, Gurney, in his wisdom, perceived that (to paraphrase yet another country song) we'd probably enjoyed as much of our night out as a couple of boys our age could stand. So we bought Mom another beer, congratulated her for having raised such a valiant and intrepid daughter, said good night, and betook ourselves home again, secure in the knowledge that, ultimately, Wonder Woman was in charge, and everything was under control.

Ken Kesey and His Kosmic Konvergence Machine

"Did you have time to learn anything?" Bud asked the young inventor.

Tom shrugged. "A little. I was using my new gadget as a wave trap or antenna to capture light of a single wave length from certain stars so I could study their red shift."

—from *Tom Swift and His Polar-Ray Dynasphere*

IN MID-NOVEMBER OF 1961, WHEN I WAS AN INSTRUCTOR in the English department of Oregon State College, in Corvallis, I got a note from a friend and fellow Kentuckian, James Baker Hall, who had been in Wallace Stegner's creative writing program at Stanford with Ken Kesey the preceding year. Kesey, Jim said, was about to publish his first novel, and had returned to his native Oregon to begin another one.

"You must go down to Springfield," Jim urged, "and meet this gregarious young genius."

Jim's suggestion got my immediate attention. For I too had once been, all too briefly, in the graduate creative writing program at Stanford, having ignominiously flunked out of same back in 1956, after only two academic quarters. I'd yearned ever since to take another shot at it, and it so happened that, to that very purpose, I was just then putting the finishing touches on the first draft of a novella that I thought might have a chance for a Stegner Fellowship. So on the day after Thanksgiving I mailed off my application to Stanford, and on Saturday, as per the arrangement I'd made with Ken by phone, I and my good friend and OSC colleague John Haislip, a promising young poet, drove down to Springfield to meet the heralded prodigy at a loggers' drinking establishment called The Spar.

I liked Ken right away—there was an openness about him, an air of amiable self-assurance that I found instantly engaging—and we soon discovered much to talk about: To my delight, the novel he was about to publish—something about a cuckoo, evidently—was dedicated to an old friend of mine, Vic Lovell, who had been my roommate during that ill-fated first adventure at Stanford. Ken and Vic (or "Vik," as Ken spelled it) had been neighbors on Perry Lane, a dusty, idyllic little Bohemian enclave near the Stanford campus, where Vic and I had often visited some rather quirky friends of ours five years ago. He and his wife, Ken said, would be moving back there in a few months; he was back in Oregon only temporarily, working off and on in the logging industry in preparation for the second novel.

And as we talked on, we found that we'd each had the happy experience of a writing workshop under the aegis of Malcolm Cowley, one of the foremost literary figures of the time, who occasionally filled in for his friend Wallace Stegner, as he'd done back in '56 and more recently in 1960, while Ken was in the program. Mr. Cowley, a noted critic and editor—it was he who resurrected William Faulkner from oblivion, when he edited *The Viking Portable Faulkner* in 1946—had treated me with cordial kindness (and considerable forbearance, unlike Stanford's less-forgiving English lit professors) when I'd been his callow student five years earlier, so naturally I thought very fondly of him—as did Ken, with good reason, considering that Mr. Cowley had championed *One Flew Over the Cuckoo's Nest* (as he had previously championed Kerouac's *On the Road*) at Viking Press, where the novel would soon be published.

After John and I had disposed of a beer or two (Ken didn't drink at all in those days), we strolled from The Spar over to the Springfield Creamery, operated by Ken's brother, Chuck, and their father, Fred, in a cavernous old building on a nearby side street. Ken gave us a quick tour of the premises—which, consistent with the nature of creameries, were somewhat steamy and humid—and as we moved along he pointed out a little heap of moldy straw in an out-of-the-way corner and mentioned, in an aside to me that I'd like to think was also a tacit recognition of a kindred spirit, that the straw harbored a promising crop of psilocybin mushrooms.

If I've got anything to say about it, I told myself on the spot, this friendship definitely has a future.

That moment proved to be prophetic, in more ways than one: Fast-forward now to Thanksgiving Day of 1962, just two days short of exactly one year into the aforementioned future, in the course of which I did win a Stegner Fellowship, I did find a house in the Perry Lane neighborhood, and I did begin what would turn out to be an enduring friendship with Ken—all in all, perhaps the single most eventful, transformative year of my life, before or since. And it wasn't even over yet. Not by a long shot, as I was about to discover.

So comes that fateful Thanksgiving Day, early evening, and I and my family and half the indigenous population of Perry Lane were lounging around the Keseys' house, recovering from a huge communal Thanksgiving feast, during which a good deal of the dinner table conversation concerned the recent chemically enhanced adventures—"trips," in the intriguing parlance of the day—that Ken and Vic and several others had been treating themselves to. Their stories, I had noted, were frequently punctuated by cries of "Too much!" and "Oh wow!" and "Far out!" from the cognoscenti in the company, and I envied their easy familiarity with both the experience and this spirited new language that described it. Accordingly, I was delighted when Ken led me to his medicine cabinet, selected a vial, and tapped a tiny tablet into my palm. "Here, take this," he said. "We're goin' to the movies."

Okay then, down the hatch. In my book *Famous People I Have Known*, I recounted the tumultuous results:

A scant few minutes later [Ken] and I and three or four other lunatics were sitting way down front in a crowded Palo Alto theater, and the opening credits of *West Side Story* were disintegrating before my eyes. "This is … CINERAMA!" roared the voice-over inside my head as I cringed in my seat. And though I stared almost unblinking at the screen for the next two hours and thirty-five minutes, I never saw a coherent moment of the movie. What I saw was a ceaseless barrage of guns, knives, policemen, and lurid gouts of eyeball-searing color, accompanied by an ear-splitting, cacophonous din, throughout which I sat transfixed with terror—perfectly immobile, the others told me afterward; stark, staring immobile, petrified, trepanned, stricken by the certainty, the absolute *certainty* that in one more instant the Authorities would be arriving to seize me and drag me up the aisle and off to the nearest madhouse. It was the distillation of all the fear I'd ever known, fear without tangible reason or cause or occasion, pure, unadulterated, abject Fear Itself, and for one hundred and fifty-five awful minutes it invaded me to the very follicles of my moustache.

Then, suddenly and miraculously, like a beacon in the Dark Night of the Soul, the words "THE END" shimmered before me on the screen. Relief swept over me, sweet as a zephyr. I was delivered. The curtain closed, the lights came up. I felt grand, triumphant—as if I'd just ridden a Brahma bull instead of a little old tab of psilocybin. If they'd turned off the lights again I'd have glowed in the dark.

Beside me, Ken stood up and stretched. "So how was it?" he inquired, grinning.

"Oh wow!" I croaked joyfully. "It was fa-a-a-r out!"

A gloriously eventful year for me, and an even more momentous one for Ken. Viking Press had published *One Flew Over the Cuckoo's Nest* (February 1962) to wide critical acclaim, and it was still selling briskly many months later. In the literary world, the book was generating lots of conversation: Its themes of rebellion and resistance made it a worthy successor to Kerouac and Burroughs and the Beats, while its keen satirical edge suggested to many critics that Kesey belonged in the company of Vonnegut and Joseph Heller and John Barth (et al.), the so-called black humorists. Then too, the novel raised serious questions about certain medical procedures—lobotomy, electroshock therapy—in the mental health field, as well as about such issues as psychiatric treatment, custodial confinement, and compulsory drug therapy, controversies that had kept the conversational pot boiling merrily. And most exciting of all, Kirk Douglas—Kirk Douglas!—had bought the stage and film rights—for eighteen grand, a princely sum!—and would be taking the lead role, that of the novel's irrepressible hero, Randle P. McMurphy, in both iterations.

Meanwhile, Ken was already deep into the second novel, *Sometimes a Great Notion*, about a family of Oregon loggers, the Stampers, and their intractably stubborn (albeit feckless) stand against union encroachment on the family's fiercely independent logging enterprise. Earlier that same fall, a clutch of us neighborhood literati and our loyal familiars had begun a sort of informal, floating salon (though none of us would've dreamed of calling it that), swapping manuscripts among ourselves and getting together every other week or so for the very satisfying purpose of reading our work aloud and complimenting each other on its felicities. (We didn't do much criticizing.) Ken invited his friend Larry McMurtry, whom he'd come to know during his own time in the Stanford writing program, and I brought in my new friend Bob Stone from the current Stanford class. Larry, who had already published his first novel, *Horseman, Pass By* (eventually to become the Paul Newman movie *Hud*), was working on a second, equally impressive novel called *Leaving Cheyenne*; and Bob had been wowing our Stanford class with the early chapters of his stunning first novel, *A Hall of Mirrors*; and Ken, of course, was humping right along with his big novel-in-progress; so on the whole, those aforementioned compliments were well deserved, and our salon was a modest success.

At one of our first sessions, Ken read the opening twenty-five or thirty manuscript pages of *Sometimes a Great Notion*, a brilliant set piece of descriptive writing in which a crowd of angry union men faces off against the Stampers across a swollen mountain stream. The intransigent, irascible Hank Stamper, head honcho of the clan, responds by dangling a severed human arm "like fish bait" above the water, the dead hand's middle finger upraised in the timeless gesture of defiance. It's a masterful beginning, certainly, but I was puzzled that the origin of the arm—Whose arm *is* that, anyhow?—remained undisclosed throughout the entire passage.

"Christ, *I* don't know," Ken answered, as if he found my question mildly exasperating. "That's why I'm writin' this book—to find out whose arm it is!"

And sure enough, the arm is left to dangle enticingly before the reader—and presumably before the author himself, as they work their separate ways through the ensuing several hundred pages of narrative backstory—like a carrot before a mule, until the provenance of the orphaned appendage is revealed near the novel's end. Creative writing teachers, take note.

During another session, this one at my house, the already fabled Neal Cassady, Kerouac's running mate of *On the Road* fame, suddenly showed up at the front door to say hello to Ken, whom he'd met in San Francisco a few days earlier and had somehow tracked to my doorstep. When I opened the door he came breezing right on in, already laying down one of his spellbinding word-jazz riffs—"just passing through, folks, my shed-yool just happened to coincide with Mr. Kesey's here, and all that redundancy as well, you understand, not to mention the works of Alfred, Lord Tennyson and the worst of the poems of Schiller, huntin' and peckin' away there as they did, except of course insofar as where you draw the line, that is, but in any case it was at Sebring, I believe, when Fangio, with the exhaust valves wide open ..."—and then blew back out again so fast we'd barely had time to process his arrival.

All right, here's another moment for those creative writing teachers to ponder: There we are, a den of scribblers, among us Ken Kesey and Larry McMurtry and Robert Stone, assembled for the solemn purpose of yammering away about fiction, when a genuine fictional hero—Dean Moriarty! In person!—suddenly materializes in our midst, and then just as suddenly departs, leaving us agog. All of us, that is, except Ken, who shrugged it off as a perfectly logical convergence, given that literary heroes would obviously have a natural affinity for a bunch of novelists. The miracle, he seemed to imply, would have been if Neal *hadn't* showed up.

And only later did it occur to me (as it has to many others) that Neal, with all his manic energy and zany intelligence and limitless line of Irish blarney, was also the living embodiment of yet another fictional hero: Randle P. McMurphy. True, Kesey wrote *Cuckoo's Nest* long before he met Cassady, but that was long *after* he'd read *On the Road* and declared himself its ardent admirer. If there were a DNA test for fictional characters, I'd bet the farm that Moriarty is McMurphy's most immediate progenitor (latest in a line of literary rogues stretching back to Falstaff and beyond)—which, in turn, would make Neal the flesh-and-blood avatar of both characters, a hipster fictional hero twice over. Then too, Neal himself was already an influential (albeit unpublished) author in his own right, having written his pal Jack the letters that inspired the "spontaneous prose" of *On the Road*, letters that would eventually find a home of their own in Neal's autobiography, *The First Third*. No wonder my little living room had begun to seem a bit crowded.

As I came to know Ken, I would learn that such cosmic, logic-defying confluences happened around him all the time, almost as if he were cloaked in some sort of invisible Tom Swiftian magnetic force field that attracted all manner of preternatural phenomena. Here, for instance, is an eye-witness account by Lee Quarnstrom—an inner-circle Prankster of the late '60s who also had a long career as a skeptical, tough-minded journalist, and who is certainly no pushover for clairvoyant hocus-pocus—describing just such an event:

> We were invited down to Asilomar, the Unitarians' Pacific
> Grove conference grounds at the point where Monterey

Bay meets the Pacific Ocean, for the church's annual retreat and whoopdeedoo. Kesey miraculously—or so it
seemed—told the enthralled Unitarians one evening to
stare out across the ocean. Something big was gonna happen, Kesey predicted, although he admitted he had no idea
what it would be. And when the last bit of the sun dipped
beneath the horizon, the sky for an instant was painted a
neon green, the so-called green flash, I believe, that people
see in Hawaii but never in California.

So had Ken somehow learned that an unprecedented
green-flash sunset was on California's meteorological docket
for that very evening (which, I'll remind you, would have
been a remarkable coincidence all by itself), and then used
the knowledge to prank his audience? Or had the flash simply
happened to coincide with the precise moment he asked the
audience to admire the sunset, just in time for him to grab the
credit for it? (Another remarkable coincidence there, of course,
but …) Surely he hadn't crowed up the flash all by himself, like
the self-important cock of post hoc infamy—or had he?

In any case, pulling off the stunt (if stunt it was) had required vast measures of sheer presence of mind, of alertness
and self-assurance and ready wit—of *cool*, if you will, in all the
myriad and varied senses of the word. And whatever else one
might have thought of Ken Kesey, I'm pretty sure anyone who
knew him would have to agree that, at a minimum, he was
very, very cool.

—

When I was in grad school back in Kentucky, I had become friends with a young history major named Pat Monaghan, who, like me, had landed in California a few years later. Pat had picked up a degree in secondary education along the way, and, by the late 1960s, was teaching social studies and drama in a large Sacramento high school; I, meanwhile, was clinging like an incubus to a "visiting" lectureship in the Stanford writing program, a post I'd held tenaciously (if tenuously) since 1963. Pat and I had soon rediscovered each other on the Left Coast and resumed our friendship, and in early 1969 Pat told me that the student drama club he sponsored at school was mounting a production of *One Flew Over the Cuckoo's Nest*.

Thanks to Tom Wolfe's immensely popular *The Electric Kool-Aid Acid Test*, there's no need to recount here what Ken had been up to during the '60s. Suffice it to say that by 1969 he had firmly taken root again on an old dairy farm back home in Oregon, having made a considerable name for himself in the interim as a Merry Prankster and menace to society and visionary performance artist and fugitive from justice and jailbird and general, all-around public character. In the course of events, *Cuckoo's Nest* (despite Kirk Douglas in the lead and Gene Wilder as Billy Bibbit and a script by *Man of La Mancha* playwright Dale Wasserman) had come and gone pretty quickly and quietly on Broadway; and *Sometimes a Great Notion*, masterpiece though it certainly is, had appeared to mixed reviews, followed by an ambitious but largely forgettable movie. Nor had Kirk Douglas found a producer for a *Cuckoo's Nest* film; rumor had it that he'd given up the project for himself, and had turned the film rights over to his son Michael, as a twenty-fifth birthday present. Meanwhile, Ken's reputation as a rising young novelist was slowly giving way to his notoriety as a writer gone rogue, and his first novel's brief turn on the stage was fast becoming a distant memory.

Still, Pat was hoping for Ken's stamp of approval on his project, and maybe even a little input from him; but, as in the ancient joke about the amorous pismire on the elephant's leg, the first order of business was to get the elephant's attention. And it just so happened—here comes that Kesey serendipity again, right on schedule—*it just so happened* that I and two other Kentucky writers, my friends Gurney Norman and Wendell Berry (both of whom were temporary transplants in the Stanford community at the time, and both of whom had befriended Ken a few years earlier, during their own sojourns in the Stegner program) were planning a pilgrimage up to Springfield to visit the Keseys at their farm. Of course we invited Pat to tag along, and arranged to pick him up as we passed through Sacramento on our way north.

Although there was precious little agriculture going on, the Kesey farm was nonetheless a very lively place just then. Ken and his family (immediate and extended) lived in a large, venerable, semi-converted dairy barn, and there seemed to be Pranksters roosting everywhere, from the cow-stall bedrooms to the hayloft, carrying on day and night in the traditional unrestrained Prankster fashion. Pat (who, thirty years later, would write an account of our trip for the posthumous final issue of Ken's magazine, *Spit in the Ocean*) found their hijinks a bit disconcerting at first, but after a day or so "I was able" (he writes) "to talk at some length with Ken, and we agreed that this play needed to be staged so as to involve the audience as much as possible, and that light projections should be used to represent Chief Bromden's musings. These projections, developed by Prankster Roy Sebern—who had literally invented the technique, back in the Perry Lane days—using overhead projectors, backlit stencils, oil paints, and food coloring, were all the rage just then at rock concerts, and the kids at my school had already experimented with them at dances and various 'happenings.'"

Buoyed by Ken's blessing, Pat went back to Sacramento full of exciting plans and ideas. He and his drama club crew designed and began building a "three-quarter round" set that would draw the audience into the action. They assembled a cast that included many of the school's misfits and miscreants in key roles, and devised a plan to coax volunteers from the audience to come onstage, don straitjackets, and assume the role of the silent "chronics" in the play. "More than three hundred students," Pat recalls, "tried out for speaking parts, silent stand-ins, technical crew, publicity, etc. ... Alienated campus rebels who had shunned any and all extra-curricular activities were camped out at the drama room door during breaks, lunch, and between classes, hoping to be part of *Cuckoo's Nest*." And, he says, "when a boy who stood about four feet tall and had a harelip and a speech defect tried out for the role of Billy Bibbit, I knew we had something special going!"

The play was a resounding success. Scheduled to run just two weekends (six performances), it racked up an unprecedented eight weekends, twenty-four performances in all. During its run Pat and I hatched various schemes to get Ken and me, separately or together, to a show, but nothing worked out. Sacramento was a long way off for either of us, and Ken, despite his earlier encouragement, seemed less than thrilled at the prospect of actually sitting through a high school performance of a play he'd probably just as soon have been allowed to forget. Finally, late in the spring, I phoned and took one last shot at persuading him, but he said sorry, he couldn't make it, he and a couple of Oregon cohorts would be going down to L.A. on some obscure Pranksterish mission for the next ten days or so, and wouldn't be available. If I wanted to hang out at the farm awhile, he added, they'd pick me up on their way back up north.

Okay, I figured, that does it; Sacramento is now out of the picture and out of the question. The school year was winding down and *Cuckoo's Nest* was closing out its run, and by the Saturday that was to mark the final performance, the whole Sacramento business had completely slipped my mind—which is to say that atmospheric conditions were ideal for a serendipity attack.

Predictably (never trust a Prankster), they showed up about a week early, around four o'clock in the afternoon on that very Saturday, at my house in Palo Alto: Ken and two latter-day compatriots, "Bobby Sky" Steinbrecher and Kathi Wagner, along with Roy Sebern, whom they had just picked up over in East Palo Alto. They'd wrapped things up in L.A. sooner than expected, they said, and they would just help themselves to a little taste of my special hospitality provisions while I got my gear together, and then we'd all be off to Oregon.

Moving fast, I threw a few things into a backpack and grabbed a sleeping bag, and then, while they were still abusing my hospitality, I ventured the observation that I-5, the interstate to Oregon, runs right past Sacramento, and Pat's play closes tonight, and wouldn't it be kind of a shame if we ...

All right, all right, Ken said at last, a bit wearily, we'll ask the Ching. Now in those days Ken and his I Ching (for the culturally disadvantaged, that's the so-called Chinese Book of Changes, which at the toss of a few coins will tell you more than you really wanted to know about what you ought to do next in whatever situation you happen to find yourself in at any given moment) were virtually inseparable; he relied on the Ching's wise counsel in all his earthly affairs—well, in most of them, at any rate. Privately, I was generally pretty skeptical of the Ching's oracular powers, but this time the ancient know-it-all was right on the money: "Go forth and see to the people at their work" (or words to that effect), the disembodied sage advised. I immediately called Pat and asked him to hold five seats for us, and we were off to Sacramento.

Ken's favorite transportation back then was an old Cadillac convertible—*any* old Cadillac convertible; as soon as he'd thoroughly worn one out, he'd find the nearest used car lot and buy another. In just such a rump-sprung, roomy old beast we lumbered our ponderous way ninety miles north and wandered aimlessly through the Sacramento backstreets until, with Prankster-perfect timing, we somehow bumbled upon Pat's school, and arrived at our seats just as the houselights went down.

The play was an authentic triumph. This was their

twenty-fourth and final performance, and Pat's unprepossessing assortment of postadolescent outlaws and outcasts were now veteran thespians playing to one last full house—and Ken Kesey was in the audience! The players had real command of their roles, the staging brought the audience all the madhouse intimacy it could stand, the casting was uniformly excellent— especially the little kid with the speech defect, who imbued the Billy Bibbit role with Dickensian poignancy—and the ingenious light-show projections added a darkly vivid, properly disorienting visual dimension to Chief Bromden's unsettling soliloquies. Roy Sebern, who sat next to me, was positively beaming through his whiskers.

"After the final curtain," Pat writes in *Spit in the Ocean*, "Kesey went up to the two leads during curtain call and hugged them. This brought the house down and, weirdly, without electrical manipulation, the lights seemed to come up brighter around them."

It's true; the audience's attention singled him out as though it were a spotlight, and lit him up like a cosmological Christmas tree. I'm trying to avoid the word "magical" (as Ken's and my old friend Paul Krassner once put it, I wouldn't want to go all misty-poo here), but in his own high school days Ken had been an amateur magician, and sometimes it almost seemed as if he must've sprinkled a little fairy dust on himself.

It wasn't magic this time, though. This time it was pure, unadulterated one hundred percent charisma.

—

While *Cuckoo's Nest* was enjoying its long run in Sacramento, it caught the attention of someone involved with an independent San Francisco theatrical troupe called the Little Fox Theater, who performed in a small, beautifully appointed venue of the same name. Unbeknownst to Pat, they sent a tech representative to see the high school production, and after it closed he received a letter from Little Fox asking permission to use some of his set and staging ideas—especially the light projections—in their own production of the play.

That production ran for the next five years, a San Francisco record that, I believe, still stands. I saw it three times myself, twice with Johnny Weissmuller Jr. as Chief Bromden. (He was terrific, by the way.) In 1971, the success of the Little Fox production begat, in its turn, an off-Broadway revival in New York with Danny DeVito and William Devane; it ran two full years and begat, in 1975, the hit motion picture, which begat a whole litter of Oscars, five in all, for Michael Douglas and company. And every single one of those little gold-plated quintuplets, friends, is the great-great-grandchild of a high school play in Sacramento back in 1969.

Even so, Ken would probably never have accepted them as real family, inasmuch as he steadfastly, resolutely—and famously—refused to see the film; he had read the script, he declared, and had realized that the movie would portray Nurse Ratched as the villain, while it let society off the hook. That didn't mean, though, that he was about to do the same for Douglas, Inc. Remember that cool eighteen grand he pocketed back in 1962, when they bought the rights? In 1975 dollars, that once-princely sum was already looking pretty measly; and compared to the kind of dough the film soon began raking in, it was downright piddling. So he sued 'em, claiming that in prior negotiations the studio had made verbal commitments to him that they failed to honor.

In the course of his Prankster exploits, Kesey had accumulated a whole phalanx of lawyers, but with neither witnesses nor a physical record of those promises, his claim was looking rather shaky ... until the night one of his sharp-eyed attorneys happened—or *just happened*, if you will—to catch Michael Douglas snappishly taking exception to the lawsuit, saying in a television interview that they had *always* intended to pay Ken the going rate. Presto! Instantly, a brand-new, ironclad verbal contract materialized before the wily young barrister's litigious eyes! Now was that mere coincidence (again), or was it ... fairy dust?

During the last year of Ken's life—2001—*Cuckoo's Nest* returned to Broadway in a revival starring Gary Sinise, the celebrated "Lieutenant Dan" of *Forrest Gump*. Ken's health was already failing, but he managed somehow to get himself to New York, and to the play. Afterward, he was taken backstage, accompanied by a *New York Times* reporter, to meet the star, who of course asked him how he'd liked the show. Well, Ken responded (to Sinise's evident displeasure), it was okay, but it wasn't his favorite.

"That designation," said the *Times*, "[Kesey] reserved for a production he saw 30 years ago at a Sacramento high school.

"'I gave that one the A,' he said.

"'Oh yeah?' Mr. Sinise replied, forcing a smile."

Straw Dog: Snarly Pete on the Ramparts

> The answer is never the answer. The need for myster-
> ies is greater than the need for answers.
>
> —Ken Kesey

ON A NARROW, LITTLE-USED SIDE STREET THAT BORDERS
my neighborhood, there squats a long, one-story concrete-
block commercial building of dismal aspect and scant
outward evidence of recent human activity of any sort whatsoever, commercial or otherwise. Massively overshadowed
by a much larger, much newer building across the street, its
unprepossessing facade is separated from the curb only by the
width of a skimpy sidewalk. The interior is divided into four
large rooms, each of which has its own doorway and its own
fairly expansive show window; otherwise, it's as windowless
as a root cellar. The roofline is low, but there's no attic, so
the ceilings are improbably high. Each doorway is protected
by a tattered, time-worn canvas awning the shape and pallor
of half a loaf of unbaked bread, a style which once bespoke,
anomalously, a swanky niteclub or a ritzy hotel, neither of

which this cheerless, woebegone old structure has ever been, or ever could become.

Yet it has, withal, a certain cachet. For many years now, I've treated myself to a daily meditative stroll around the neighborhood, but so profound was the old hulk's glum anonymity that it was years before I noticed that because the side street isn't perpendicular to the main drag it feeds into, the building (therefore) isn't rectangular, but rather an elongated parallelogram. (Small wonder I flunked plane geometry.) Accordingly, the four rooms inside it are also parallelograms—as I discovered by stopping from time to time to peer voyeuristically through the dust-coated windows. Inside, the long walls of each room angle off crazily to the left, as though the entire building had been wrenched askew, "sprung" somehow, like the hood of a car after a fender bender. Even on the sunniest days, precious little daylight penetrates the gloom. Standing before one of those wide, murky windows, I found, was like standing at the mouth of a cave, the emptiness within looming vast and dark, unfathomed.

But before it was dwarfed by its relatively monumental new neighbor, this concrete bunker was probably the most imposing building on the street. I can imagine it brand new in the postwar 1940s, four nice hopeful little shoppes all in a row—a Western Auto store, say, and maybe a carpet store, and a five-and-dime, and a modern-as-tomorrow beauty parlor. It would have been an embryonic mini-mall, trying desperately, with its toney awnings and venturesome, futuristic interior angles, to be classy, up-town, the Latest Thing.

Twenty-five years ago, when I first took root as an invasive species in these environs, the old building still had a couple of tenants—one elderly gent reconditioned grandfather clocks, another performed the same service for old vacuum-tube radios—but for self-evident reasons neither enterprise seemed destined to prosper, and within the next few years first one, then the other closed, and the place stood empty. For a very long time thereafter, the only thing that ever seemed to change—and this only every couple of years or so—was the identity of whichever local realtor was currently posting For Sale signs in the windows.

At this juncture of my narrative, on the probably erroneous assumption that among my readers there might be some benighted wretch who doesn't have the good fortune, or good sense, to live in Lexington, Kentucky, as I do, I have to interrupt myself just long enough to explain that among the very top ranks of deceased Lexington icons—such as Henry Clay and Adolph Rupp and Little Enis, the World's Greatest Left-Handed Upside-Down Guitar Player—is one Smiley Pete, a nondescript little spotted dog who roamed the downtown streets back in the 1950s, making himself at home at any number of business establishments. In the course of a day, old Pete might pay social calls at a newsstand, a couple of cafés, a shoe repair shop, a barber shop, a dry cleaner, even a law office or two, collecting treats and tributes at every stop like a furry little gunsel in a gangster movie, making his rounds and marking his territory on fire hydrants and lampposts along the way, smiling throughout as amiably as a crocodile. Smiley Pete's long gone, of course, but he lives on in Lexington's civic memory, immortalized by a commemorative plaque downtown and, eponymously, by Smiley Pete Publishing, the publisher of our thriving monthly community magazine, the *Chevy Chaser*, where he also serves as spiritual mascot and logo.

Okay, back to Our Story Thus Far: So if you walk around behind the east end of that grim old building of mine (and yes, I'm declaring a proprietary interest there, although I have no idea who actually holds the deed), you will find yourself standing at the head of a short blind alley that immediately narrows to a dank, forbidding concrete block passageway, and dead-ends abruptly at a block wall, upon which an unknown hand has painted an almost-but-not-quite-successful trompe l'oeil photorealistic representation of a medium-large spotted dog in full attack mode, ears laid back, fangs bared, poised to leap. Above him to the left, on a barred window that looks like it could be an aperture into a jail cell, is a BEWARE OF DOG sign; to the right, padlocked, is the back door of the building.

I first encountered this slavering Cerberus shortly after I moved into the neighborhood, when, walking home from a downtown bar late one bibulous evening, I stepped into that alleyway for purposes familiar to every late-night tippler, and was going about my affairs in a relaxed but businesslike manner when I glanced up to see—Egad!—a mad dog rushing at me out of the darkness!

Now some persons in my condition would have been unnerved by this development, and taken flight, but not me, no buddy; I stood my ground before the ravenous brute, and befriended him, and when I appropriated the building I appropriated him as well. Snarly Pete, I calls him, and although he doesn't answer to the name, his loyalty and steadfastness are unparalleled. His paint is peeling, and he's slowly fading into oblivion as the years go by, but under Snarly's watchful eye— which, by the way, proves on close inspection to be curiously and unaccountably star-shaped—my building has remained unmolested. Stubbornly defying the passage of time, it stands unaltered in its quintessential homeliness.

During a walk one day about three years ago, I was startled out of my perambulatory musings to find a dump truck and a front-end loader in the narrow street, and several workmen with sledgehammers industriously punching a great, gaping hole smack in the middle of the front of my building. A couple of days later, the opening had been neatly trimmed out and closed off by an overhead garage door, the workmen and the heavy equipment were gone, and all was serene again. And so it remained for three more years.

This past December, a capacious Dumpster suddenly materialized one day in front of my building, and workmen were once again scurrying to and fro, some humping great slabs of moldy old drywall and ceiling tile and splintery plywood to the Dumpsters while others raised a tremendous racket hammering and sawing and ripping and tearing inside. Over the following couple of days the crew hauled away two or three Dumpsterloads of deconstruction debris. Yet after they'd stripped the walls and ceilings to the studs and hauled away the last load, I peered in through one of the grimy windows and saw that, inexplicably, everything looked more or less the same as it had looked before: still cavernous and shrouded in gloom, still empty but for a few abandoned reminders of the workers' recent exertions—here a sawhorse, there an overturned bucket, way off in the far corner an upended wheelbarrow leaning on its handles—still vaguely sinister, and just as inscrutable as ever.

Finally, late one afternoon not long ago, I found that parties unknown had left an auto transport trailer parked where the Dumpster used to be, and on the trailer was an old automobile covered by a tarp. I thought I recognized the car's distinctive, snout-nosed profile, and since there was no one around, I took the liberty of lifting the skirt of the tarp (I used the tip of my cane, shameless old roué that I am) and sneaking a peek at its ample rear end. Sure enough, it was a 1956 Studebaker Golden Hawk, a car I had briefly admired, in my callow youth, for its snazzy, fin-bedizened, pseudo-futuristic styling. From what I could see, the old banger—a coupe in the body style once known as "hard-top convertible," with side windows that opened all the way back—was in pretty good condition; its once-glowing golden paint job had gone all dingy and ocherous, and the chrome was pocked with rust, but it was still on its wheels, and it looked to be intact all the way around; even the taillights were unbroken.

As I moved along, I was already saluting the cosmic agencies, whatever they may be, that brought together these two venerable relics, the cockeyed building and the misbegotten automobile, at this late stage of their respective inanimate lives. They belong together, it seemed to me; they complete and complement each other perfectly. Next day, the transport trailer was gone, and another bit of stealthy window-peeping revealed that the car was now inside—presumably via the garage door that's awaited it for three years now. Divested of the tarp, the Studebaker hunkered contentedly in the shadowy recesses of the furthermost corner of its gloomy chamber—where, incidentally, it rests to this very day, as though it has found a haven at last.

Of course, if I were so inclined, I could just walk on down to city hall some afternoon and find out who actually pays taxes on the property (certainly not me), and then a couple more blocks to the public library—in the heart of Smiley Pete's old territory—where an hour or so of research would surely yield all there is to know about the building's brief and probably mundane history.

But those are facts, and "facts" are exactly what I don't want to know, inasmuch as they will inevitably get in the way of the little fictions I've enjoyed telling myself during my walks for most of the last twenty-five years. Facts have nothing to do with the fanciful scenarios that I entertain—and that entertain me—when I pass the building in the course of my daily trudgery. Rather, my speculations tend to be of an existential character, and they often assume a somewhat fuzzy, disjointed visual dimension as well, like random pages from a poorly drawn graphic novel. So:

Did Smiley Pete himself ever wander up this way and frequent these old shoppes? Does he still haunt the premises, or did that upstart Snarly run him off? Is this place futuristic, or medieval? In the dead of night, when there's nobody around to hear them, does it resonate with the chimes of ancient grandfather clocks, the crackling voices of old-time radio? Whence cometh those anomalous awnings? Is that a jail cell … or a dungeon? A torture chamber, even? Whose dog *is*

Snarly Pete, if not mine? That black star in his eye, could that be some creepy, cultish symbol, a curse, a warning that something wicked is afoot? Is that a theremin I hear?

And now, with the advent of the mysterious Studebaker, my building has become the secret lair of ... um—yes!—of HawkDude ("Hawkman" being taken, let's go with something more contemporary), crusading crime fighter, half man, half bird of prey, scourge of evildoers throughout the Bluegrass and the entire Tri-County Area! He roosts up there in the rafters until the instant his natural hawkish super senses kick in and alert him that criminal activity is afoot in our fair city, whereupon the Hawkster coolly folds his wings and drops like a plumb bob, slap into the driver's seat of the Studebaker— that unpromising conveyance having, in the meantime, conveniently metamorphosed from crusty old over-designed rustbucket into, hey, this sleek, elongated twenty-four-karat-gold-plated top-down imaginary convertible roadster version of its former clunky self, and it awaits him with its 285-horse V-8 engine already rumbling, pulsing in readiness beneath its gleaming, golden hood!

Then HawkDude—a handsome chap despite his steely-eyed but disfiguring squint and the cruel, hooked scimitar of a beak that divides his feathered countenance—HawkDude clutches the steering wheel with taloned fists and revs the V-8 to a fearsome crescendo and scratches off in true studly HawkDude fashion, even as the garage door rolls up with split-second open-sesame precision just in time and just far enough for the Stoodie—let's assign the intrepid chariot a gender, and call her Gilda—to rocket through the opening,

HawkDude at the wheel with that fierce beak preceding him as though it were his own personal hood ornament, his loyal canine companion Snarly Pete riding shotgun with his shaggy head lolling out doggy-like on the passenger side, and now Gilda spreads her gilt-tipped wings—formerly her '56 Studebaker tailfins—and away they roar into the night while all the tiny local malfeasants and malefactors scurry for their hidey-holes …

Well, y'know, it's really kind of wonderful how far a person's imagination can take him when he's trying to put off doing his income taxes. But I do have one more brief tale of supernatural hanky-panky in connection with my building, and then I'll hush:

Recently, a new, aggressively large FOR LEASE sign has appeared, draped along the building's parapet, and I suspect that change is on the way, and that Snarly Pete's days are probably numbered. So, lest his memory be lost forever in the mists of time, I suggested to my photographer friend Guy Mendes— who shares, in his work, my own affinity for eccentric (some would say oddball) subjects (I happen to be one of them)— that he might find Snarly both compelling and, in a noirish sort of way, quite photogenic.

The afternoon Snarly Pete sat (as it were) for *Beware of Dog*—Guy's perfect portrait of him that embellishes and graces this story—turned out to be unseasonably cold and blustery and bleak, the perfect atmospherics for what we had in mind but not the sort of day that invites a lot of foot traffic; the wind was sharp and bitter and there wasn't a living soul in sight. We left the car in front of the building and were walking around to the back for our rendezvous with Snarly, when we heard a vaguely familiar *Thwup! Thwup! Thwup!* coming down the street toward us. A basketball! Bouncing merrily along all by itself straight down the middle of the street as though a ghostly point guard had just come into the game! And it bounded right past us as we stood there gaping, and as it passed it seemed to be shrinking somehow, getting smaller with every *thwup,* smaller and smaller until it was no bigger than an orange, and then it suddenly veered left and *thwup-thwup-thwip-thwip* bounced straight down a storm drain and disappeared forever!

Cue the theremin, and fade to black.

Coda: I didn't tell Guy about HawkDude and Gilda and the evildoers; there are certain things a person really ought to keep to himself. But anyone who doubts me about that spectral basketeer should just ask Guy, who before he became a hippie photographer was a walk-on UK Wildkitten (he made the freshman traveling squad in 1967), and wouldn't lie about such a matter under any circumstances, lest Adolph Rupp rise from the grave and smite him a good one.

The World's Greatest Fungo Hitter

Ruminations on Memory, Mortality, and the Cincinnati Reds

Sensible as I am

of the honor conveyed

by your invitation

I cannot accept

because I am dead

(Tra-la).

—WENDELL BERRY,

"At Last a Good Excuse"

ALTHOUGH I'M STILL A RESIDENT KENTUCKIAN, I HAVEN'T lived in Bracken County since 1948, just before I turned sixteen. Nonetheless, I'm a longtime subscriber and devoted reader of the weekly *Bracken County News*, which I search assiduously each week for names I remember from my childhood. On a map of Kentucky large enough and detailed enough to show the state's hundred and twenty individual counties, Bracken would be a tiny patch of geography about the size of your thumbnail, tucked into a sweeping northward bend of the Ohio River just west of Maysville, forty-some-odd miles southeast of Cincinnati. It's a small, rural county with, even now, a relatively stable population, so my scrutiny of the obits in the *News* is often rewarded with a spark or two of recognition. If some old boyhood friend or acquaintance hasn't died, one might turn up among the pallbearers, or in the lists of the bereaved or—more and more routinely nowadays—the predeceased.

After I've exhausted the entertainment value of that melancholy pursuit, I usually console myself by turning to the column called "Tabitha's Tidbits," a compilation of odds and ends from the depths of the *News*'s back-issues morgue, which often proves the ideal antidote for an overdose of gloom. Tabitha, bless her pseudonymous heart, has been electing lately to reprint old "Social Notes" columns chronicling the antic doings of Bracken society in 1903. In the last couple of issues, scattered among items ranging in newsworthiness from "Miss Susie Norris of Minerva spent Saturday and Sunday with Miss Anna Boyd in Brooksville" to "Isaac Disher of Needmore delivered a nice bunch of heifers to Harbin Moore at Chatham," I've come across such delectable observations as "We are sorry the blackberry crop is about over, for there will be nowhere to go"; and "R. R. Colter was in Cincinnati last week and he bought a whole train of goods. That's the way he buys"; and my favorite, "The fair sex of Wellsburg take great delight in sitting on the veranda on Sunday afternoons watching the rubber buggies as they whiz along, saying only 'It might have been.'"

Stella Yelton McClanahan, my paternal grandmother, who in 1903 would have been a young wife and mother in Johnsville, just down the road from Wellsburg, would almost certainly have been acquainted socially with the wistful maidens on that veranda; indeed, in the not very distant past, she too had doubtless spent a few Sunday afternoons ensconced on her daddy's veranda, making eyes at the young bucks whizzing along in their sporty new rubber-tired rigs.

Stella—"Mom Mack," I called her—lived to be ninety-two years old. By the time I came along in 1932, she was already, by prevailing standards, "getting up in years," and as I was growing up I always thought of her as a very old lady. Yet although I was to know her throughout the last thirty-five years or so of her life (and the first thirty-five of mine), she never really seemed to grow the least bit older—an illusion nurtured in part by her meek but steadfast refusal to tell anyone how old she was. Age, in her opinion, was strictly a private matter; she'd no more have disclosed her birthday—or celebrated it— than she'd have stood up in church and announced the current condition of her underwear. (I seem to recall that when she died, they'd had to consult a family Bible to determine her age for the death certificate.) So in a sense, she was both aged and ageless, eternally the same affectionate, timorous little soul, fretful yet as chipper and cheerful as a songbird—whose favorite diversion, nonetheless, was going to funerals.

The younger members of Mom Mack's family, my half-baked self among them, were inclined to make light of her gloomy but endearing pastime—it seemed, on the one hand, faintly ghoulish, and, on the other, absurdly quaint and old-timey—but now that the years have brought me to the point where every day is a whole new adventure in longevity, I like to picture my sweet old granny flitting from funeral to funeral like a lachrymose little butterfly, tenderly dispensing sympathy among the mourners as though she were anointing them with her tears—as perhaps, indeed, she was.

Mom Mack lived all but the last few of her ninety-two years in Bracken County, in a succession of modest houses in Johnsville, Chatham, and Brooksville, always under the same roof as her bachelor brother, my great uncle Cliff Yelton. Like his sister, Uncle Cliff—"Unk"—had always seemed to me preternaturally ancient, as though he'd been old right from the get-go, and had just stayed that way. Come to think of it, I'm not even sure which sibling was the eldest; they might've been twins for all I knew—both had sandy hair, and both were prone to freckle—except that Mom Mack was frail and wispy, whereas Unk was a portly gent, as round and solid as a croquet ball. Still, they complemented each other perfectly in at least one important respect: Mom Mack was a fabulous cook, and Unk had a prodigious appetite.

Heavy feeder though he was, Unk had never really done much to earn his keep. My grandfather Claude, a farmer, sometime tobacco speculator, and (I think) Johnsville dry goods merchant, died before my second birthday, and during the earliest years of my childhood Mom Mack and Unk continued to live on the small family farm in the hills just outside Johnsville. Unk took care of the chickens and gardened a little, and he had probably helped out in the store now and then before the Depression shut it down; but otherwise (as Wendell

Berry once said of a fellow we both knew) "he always did the minimum."

Despite his torpid nature, Unk had possessed, in his time, a unique athletic talent: He'd been, according to my dad, the world's greatest fungo hitter—or, at any rate, Johnsville's greatest fungo hitter. In the ancient game of baseball, see, a fungo hitter is the gent who stands at home plate during pregame practice and hits grounders to the infielders and fly balls to the outfielders. And of course, like any other human activity that requires a modicum of physical dexterity, there's an art to it. A good fungo hitter, no matter how cumbersome and ungainly he may be in other walks of life, performs at the plate with the languid, effortless grace of a well-oiled automaton, tossing the ball up and swatting it in what almost seems a single motion, tirelessly spraying hits hither and yon about the playing field with lazy, masterful precision. Doing it well requires good hand-eye coordination but very little physical exertion, and Unk, it seemed, was adequately equipped in the former department and naturally gifted in the latter.

Unk's fungo-hitting days were already far behind him during my boyhood, but he had never lost his enthusiasm for the National Pastime—especially insofar as the game was executed and embodied by his heroes, the Cincinnati Reds. The Reds were a rising team in the late 1930s, and in 1940 (the year I turned eight) they won the World Series for the first time since 1919, when the infamous Chicago Black Sox rolled over and played dead for them. Unk religiously followed the fortunes of the resurgent Reds in the *Cincinnati Enquirer*, and listened raptly to the play-by-play of every game on the armoire-sized Silvertone radio in Mom Mack's parlor, with his rocking chair on its tiptoes and his best ear close to the speaker.

Now I'd been chronically puny as a small child, and during my periodically recurrent downtime, radio had been my boon companion. I was very fond of stories in general at that age, and my indefatigable little table-model Crosley (a modern wonder compared to Unk's big old static-spitting Silvertone) told me an enchanting assortment of them all afternoon long, steeping my small-fry person day after day in the steamy affairs of Our Gal Sunday and Young Widder Brown and Ma Perkins. By about the age of six or seven, I had begun to outgrow my weanling puniness, and as I became more robust, and belatedly started school, I was obliged to forego my afternoon dalliance with the soap opera ladies. But I still hurried home in time to catch Jack Armstrong and the Lone Ranger and Lum and Abner, and my devotion to radio continued unabated. The stories my Crosley told seemed almost more real than the world around me, the story I was living.

My parents were both employed, so when school was out I was often remanded to the custody of one or the other of my grandmothers—which suited me fine, by the way, since either of those forbearing old dears was always good for a second helping of dessert, or just about any other indulgence I required. And at Mom Mack's, I could pal around with Unk, who wasn't the liveliest of playmates—indeed, he was by nature both taciturn and essentially immobile—but who kindly did his level best to entertain me with riddles and tongue twisters and little tricks like producing nickels from my ears, or rolling a fifty-cent piece across his knobby old knuckles. Sometimes, after school or in the summer, I'd find myself in Unk's company when he was listening to the Reds. At first, I either read a comic book or toddled off in search of something else to do, but finally, in the summer of 1940—the year they won the Series—with the radio insisting that I pay attention to it, and the Reds enjoying a phenomenal season, and the World's Greatest Fungo Hitter sitting right beside me, eager, in his ponderous, phlegmatic way, to explain the finer points of the game, I put my comic book aside at last and started tuning in.

Unk had his favorite players, and soon enough they became my favorites too. Unk's personal hero was the great right-handed sinker-ball pitcher Bucky Walters. I had no idea what a sinker ball was, but Unk declared—in whispers, so Mom Mack wouldn't hear—that ol' Buck's was "a pisser," and that was good enough for me. We were both partial, me and Unk, to Johnny "Double No-Hit" Vander Meer, whose very nickname bespoke his ironclad claim on immortality, and also to the outsized first baseman Frank McCormick, who in my mind loomed *literally* larger than life, like Paul Bunyan or Frankenstein, or Goliath of Sunday School repute. Then too, Unk really liked the star catcher Ernie Lombardi, Unk himself having thought seriously about becoming a great catcher before he found his true calling as a fungo hitter; whereas I admired the Reds' ace right-hander Paul Derringer, mainly because I associated his name with cowboy movies, and that deadly little pistol the dangerous city slicker with the pencil-line moustache always packed, in some secret location on or about his wily person. I remember feeling vaguely disappointed when I discovered that Paul didn't sport a moustache.

Walters, Vander Meer, McCormick, Lombardi, Derringer; names to conjure with. Although of course I didn't know this yet, they were to be the nucleus of an ever-growing Reds roster that exists only in my own disorderly memory, an irregular mental record book, if you will, of indelible Reds' moments that has reconstituted and refreshed itself constantly throughout the ensuing seventy-some-odd baseball seasons, and continues to do so right up to today, right up to this very afternoon in the late summer of 2016, right up to half an hour ago, when the thrillingly fleet-footed Billy Hamilton stole home in the ninth to beat the Milwaukee Brewers 1–0 just as I was writing the first sentence of this paragraph.

In 1947, my dad took me to a Reds game at Crosley Field in Cincinnati, and Ewell "The Whip" Blackwell pitched a no-hitter; in 1978, I took my son Jess and his sister Cait to a Reds game at Riverfront Stadium in Cincinnati, and Tom "The Franchise" Seaver pitched a no-hitter. And I'd venture to say—think of this!—that I am the only person now walking the face of the earth who was present at both occasions.

Nonetheless, despite having lived most of my undeservedly durable life within a couple of hours of Cincinnati, I probably haven't seen, in the flesh, a grand total of more than twenty-five or thirty Reds' games, all but a handful of them between 1945 and 1955, and only one in the New Millennium. (I don't remember who they played, but the Reds' stylish new high-kicking right-hander Bronson Arroyo got the win.) So I can't even claim to have been an especially devoted fan, yet the sheer longevity of my enthusiasm, I hope, mitigates its lapses. In the course of those seventy-five seasons I've whiled

away untold jillions of hours listening to the Reds on radio or
watching them on television or scouring the sports pages in
some exotic foreign port such as Missoula, Montana, or Palo
Alto, California, looking for the latest box score. I suppose I'm
a Reds fan in the same sense that I'm a Merry Prankster: I
didn't do much to deserve the honorific, but—exactly as the
I Ching assures us—perseverance furthered, and I became a
Prankster (and a Reds fan) willy-nilly.

Looking back, I visualize my enduring affection for the
Reds as a wide nightscape illumined by incandescent memories beyond number, flickering randomly, like fireflies. "Highlights," the sportscasters aptly dub them, and of course in my
case they tend to come with subsidiary memories attached. At
the top of my list of Reds' highlights would necessarily have to
be seeing those two no-hitters thirty-one years apart, but that
happenstance brooks no elaboration, whereas my personal favorites require great, heaping dollops of embellishment—fair
warning, if one was needed, that I'm in my anecdotage, and
can't help it.

When I was in college in southern Ohio (this would have
been in the spring of 1954), I persuaded a young lady named
Betsy to accompany me to Cincinnati on a Greyhound bus for
a Reds game at old Crosley Field, the last game, as it happened,
that I would ever see there. Wally Post won that game for the
Reds with a homer in the eighth, and after the game Betsy and
I had a romantic dinner in a secluded booth at a dark, slightly
sinister speakeasy-style bistro called, I believe, The Barn, in a
back alley just off Vine Street. Betsy had a Tom Collins, and
I managed to choke down, without visibly wincing, the first

martini of my young life. (The second one, I might add, went
down a whole lot easier.) As for the late-night bus ride back to
campus, I won't claim that, like the redoubtable Wally, I hit a
home run ... but I did get to first base!

Now that's what I call a highlight. Here's another:

In 1990 the Reds led the National League West wire to
wire, and beat the Pirates handily in the playoffs; the Oakland
A's, meanwhile, had been even more dominant in the American League, and a great World Series was in prospect. But my
own summer had begun with a domestic cataclysm, and in
early October I was at home in Kentucky, still up to my eye-
balls in the Slough of Despond—when I unexpectedly landed
a coveted magazine assignment, and suddenly I was winging
my way to Oregon to rendezvous with my old friends Ken Kesey and the Pranksters. To my dismay, however, all the mis-
eries and megrims that bedeviled me in Kentucky had stowed
away on that same flight, infesting my woebegone person like
those hideous little fungoids that regale themselves under
people's toenails in the television commercials. I arrived at the
Keseys' on the eve of the World Series, down in the mouth to
a disfiguring degree.

The entire West Coast, I soon discovered, was uniformly
gaga over the Oakland A's. All my sporting friends out there in
darkest Oregon apparently knew only that Cincinnati was located somewhere in the Effete East, which they naturally held
in great disdain, and they were all supremely confident—not
to say smug—in the assumption that the A's would win the
Series in a cakewalk, exactly as the oddsmakers were almost
unanimously predicting. Truth to tell, I'd been too distracted

that summer to pay proper attention to the Reds' triumphant season; nonetheless, this cavalier dismissal of them so affronted my honor as a native son of the Tri-State Area, that when my longtime Prankster pal Ken Babbs proposed that we hazard a fifth of Scotch on the outcome, I intrepidly took up the gauntlet, very much against my better judgement.

Of course it turned out that my better judgment had its tiny head wedged. To the utter astonishment of the known world, myself certainly included, the Reds won that Series in four straight games. We watched it all on Kesey's TV (station KEZI, naturally), and my spirits rose ever so slightly with each win. After the final game Babbs paid up promptly, like the gentleman he is, and then he and I, working as a team, polished off that fifth in a single sitting. All in all, it was the first good time I'd allowed myself to have in many months, and later, looking back, I entertained the delicious fantasy that the Reds had done it just for me.

One more highlight, please, Ed, just one more!

Okay, since I insist, one more: For a couple of seasons in the late 1940s, the Reds employed a journeyman infielder named Jimmy Bloodworth, the grizzled veteran of a dozen major league seasons although something of banjo hitter. I'd seen his picture on the sports page; he was a ruggedly handsome guy, well into his thirties, with prematurely white hair and eyebrows as black as a pair of andirons, like Hopalong Cassidy's.

So it comes to pass that in the final hour of a sweltering, steamy summer evening in the dog days of 1949, I'm at the wheel of my mom's still-new Chevy sedan, happily

chauffeuring myself home from a profoundly gratifying little
late-date assignation with my secret extracurricular squeeze
Yvonne (whose dropout boyfriend Tommy, a coal-truck
driver, has gone to the mountains on his weekly run), and
I'm easing the Chevy through downtown Maysville with all
the windows and wind wings open wide, catching the breeze,
cooling my still somewhat dampish young self while simultaneously airing out the backseat after the divertissements that
Yvonne and I, in accordance with the imperatives of youth,
enjoyed only minutes ago in that cozy accommodation. My
heart, needless to say, is high.

On the Chevy's radio, Waite Hoyt is describing what will
shortly be the conclusion of a long, desultory Reds game with
the Chicago Cubs, their only serious rival for last place in the
National League in what has already been, for both teams, a
long, desultory season. The Reds are batting, it's the bottom
of the ninth, score tied at something like 8–8, two outs, run-
ners on second and third—and here comes creaky old Jimmy
Bloodworth to the plate! Of course Jimmy's no great threat,
but the pitcher's due up next, so the Cubbies are electing to
pay old Jim the rare compliment of walking him intentionally.
Waite's familiar creamy-smooth radio voice—in concert with
my own imagination—brings everything before my eyes with
a clarity no television will ever match. The catcher comes out
of his crouch and indicates where he expects to receive the
pitch—chin-high, and a foot and a half outside—while Jimmy
waits, patient and imperturbable, the bat resting on his shoulder. The pitcher pantomimes a full wind-up and indolently
lobs the ball in the general direction of the targeted area,

where it arrives in the catcher's mitt with a dispirited plop. "Ball one!" the umpire cries. Jimmy's watchful old eyes narrow; he appreciates the free pass, but he just don't care for this pitcher's laxy-daisy attitude somehow. As the next pitch sails past, he notes that its trajectory brings it just a *leetle* closer to him, perhaps, than the nonchalant pitcher intended. The bat twitches involuntarily on Jimmy's shoulder, as though it has a will of its own, but "That ain't my style," old Jimbo tells himself. "Ball two!" cries the ump. The third pitch comes floating in as big as a cantaloupe, a scant six inches outside the strike zone and slow enough that Jimmy can practically read the Rawlings trademark, so slow it seems almost to levitate before him like a thought balloon in the funny papers, fairly begging him to take a whack at it ... which, this time, he does, with impunity. He leans over the plate and swings with his arms extended, and the tip of his bat meets the ball a hairsbreadth short of the catcher's mitt and loops a soft, low-hanging liner just over the startled first baseman's outstretched glove and into short right field. The runner on third crosses the plate standing up ... and this one belongs to the Reds!

It was surely the capstone of Jimmy Bloodworth's diligent, worthy, largely unsung career, his payoff in glory for laboring season after season in the inescapable shadows of more gifted players. I'm sure there have been other instances of batters working a base hit out of an intentional pass, but I've yet to hear of one, and I hope I never do. (In any case, it can never happen again, the ritual acting-out of the intentional pass having recently been deemed too tedious for television.) In *my* experience, at any rate, Jimmy's stroke of genius stands alone, and I'd sort of like to keep it that way. And because it happened within the very hour of my own initial visit to the Promised Land ("I'm afraid I wasn't very good at it," I confessed to Yvonne many years later, at a high school reunion. "No," she said, "but didn't we have fun!"), from that night forward I've associated the modest heights Yvonne and I scaled with Jimmy Bloodworth's sudden elevation to the ranks of the Obscure Immortals. As to the latter, I daresay I'm once again the only living being on the planet who would claim (who would bother to claim) to have been "present" (via Waite Hoyt) for Jimmy's singular exploit *even as it was transpiring*; indeed that I'm probably the only one—the only one!—who remembers that it happened at all. Which is as it should be, I suppose, because not even immortality lasts forever.

Baseball begets stories the way a hen lays eggs; they just keep coming and coming—and when they hatch, every one of them is already kin to all the others, and to all the eggs and all the hatchlings yet to come. The manager of the Reds on the night Jimmy B. pulled off his little miracle was none other than Bucky Walters—he of the pisser of a sinker ball, Unk's hero of the 1940 World Series—and still on the Reds' roster, rounding out their illustrious careers, were both Double-No-Hit Johnny and Ewell the Whip—the latter of whom, in his next outing after the no-hitter I personally witnessed with my fourteen-year-old eyes, took his own second straight no-hitter into the ninth before it got away from him.

Speaking of radios (we were speaking of radios, weren't we?), the little table-model Crosley on which I heard Waite describe Ewell the Whip's two-hit tragedy, the very same radio that used to bring Young Widder Brown to my bedside when I was stricken with chronic puniness, was manufactured by a Cincinnati industrialist named Powel Crosley Jr., the owner of, yes, the Cincinnati Reds, which is why they played their games in a stadium called Crosley Field, where, in 1951, I saw Cannonball Kenny Raffensberger throw a one-hitter to beat the Cardinals 1–0 on a homer by Ted Kluzewski in the bottom of the eighth …

So everything connects to everything else, and for all we know, when Jimmy fixed his keen old eye on that fat pitch hanging there before him and delicately flicked it into right field, he might have been channeling Unk, the World's Greatest Fungo Hitter. And speaking of Unk (see how this works?), I'm beginning to suspect that maybe the old rascal wasn't always quite as dormant as I'd supposed. Here's a late news flash from "Tabitha's Tidbits," dateline 1903:

"Miss Pauline Knoblach of New York City, a guest of the Misses Perkins of Needmore, was seen out driving last Sunday with Mr. Clifford Yelton of Johnsville."

Reading that, I like to imagine Unk in the bloom of youth, a stocky, ruddy-faced young chap nicely turned out in his Sunday best seersucker—topped off, you may be sure, by a white straw boater—driving a high-stepping mare as she draws his smart new rubber-tired shay through sleepy downtown Johnsville on a summer Sunday afternoon, with the fetching Miss Knoblach of New York City at his side. At the edge of town there's a wide meadow, carefully mowed, where a little flock of boys of various sizes are at play on a rudimentary baseball field. Young Unk pulls up his rig in the shade of a spreading

chestnut tree just outside the first-base line, steps down and
tips his boater to Miss Knoblach by way of excusing himself
for a moment, then turns and strides purposefully across the
field toward home plate as the players cheer him on, crying,
"Fungos! Fungos! Hit us some fungos, Cliff!" Obliging them,
he picks up a bat, tucks it under his arm while he spits into
his palms and rubs them together briskly, takes a couple of
leisurely practice swings, adjusts the lapels of his Sunday suit
and the tilt of the straw boater upon his burnished brow, then
signals at last that he's ready for the ball. A nearby urchin
underhands it to him (this would be an old-time cartoony
baseball, a kids' beat-up old baseball with busted stitches
and the requisite loose flap, like the one Li'l Abner used to
toss around); but, instead of catching it, the World's Greatest Fungo Hitter draws a bead on the ungainly spheroid as it
comes flippety-flapping toward him and seizes his own Jimmy
Bloodworth moment and uncorks a mighty swing and knocks
the cover off it. Literally knocks the goddamn cover off! The
lop-eared old ball seems almost to explode off the bat; the flap-
ping cover drops away, an empty husk, as the naked roll of
twine that formed its core ascends in a towering, majestic arc
toward the deepest part of center field, unwinding itself all the
way, an ever-lengthening strand of twine trailing as the ball
itself gets smaller and smaller and teenier and tinier until—
pffft!—it simply vanishes into the pale blue sky and leaves the
spent string drifting slowly back to earth, while Miss Knoblach applauds prettily, and waves her hankie.

Well, okay, I'm fairly sure that never really happened—but
that's the way it *should* have happened, because we all deserve

to be, at least once, the hero of our own story. And it *could've* happened that way, too, because this is baseball we're talkin' here, and as we have seen, improbable stuff happens all the time in baseball. It's the nature of the game.

Acknowledgments

Portions of this book previously appeared in *North of Center, Oxford American,* and *Critical Insights: One Flew Over the Cuckoo's Nest* (Salem Press, 2015). "A Work of Genius" has also been published by Larkspur Press, in a limited edition with six woodcut illustrations by Wesley Bates.

The author wishes to thank Wesley Bates, Guy Mendes, and "Primitivo" (whoever and wherever he may be) for their works of art, and Tom Marksbury and KC for their persevering help and steadfast friendship.

© Guy Mendes

ED McCLANAHAN, a native of northeastern Kentucky, is the author of several books, including *The Natural Man* and *Famous People I Have Known*. He is the recipient of a Wallace Stegner Fellowship, two Yaddo fellowships, and an Al Smith Fellowship. He has taught at Oregon State University, Stanford University, the University of Kentucky, the University of Montana, and Northern Kentucky University. He lives in Kentucky with his wife. Find out more at edmcclanahan.com.